Eugene

&

The Haunted Train Bridge

Eugene

&

The Haunted Train Bridge

By

John William McMullen

Bird Brain Publishing

Bird Brain Publishing
Evansville, Indiana

Bird Brain Publishing is an imprint of Bird Brain Productions.

www.birdbrainproductions.com
www.birdbrainpublishing.com

The text of this book is set in Perpetua font
Cover photo by Artistic Imagery Photography, Evansville, Indiana. Additional photos by Ron L. McMullen and John W. McMullen

Library of Congress Cataloging-in-Publication Data
McMullen, John William
  Eugene & the Haunted Train Bridge / by John William McMullen
          Summary: Set in 1981 during the last week of summer vacation, Eugene Thomas dares Lambert McChesney and his adolescent peers to walk across the alleged haunted railroad bridge in the middle of the night.

  ISBN: 978-0-9826255-0-7

Printed in the United States of America

To order additional copies of this book, contact:
Bird Brain Publishing at www.birdbrainpublishing.com

For

Joe McMullen

Love covers a multitude of sins.
1 Peter 4:8

Sunrise

Crickets chirp
while the robin leads the morning chorus of birds
in a symphony of praise.
Slowly the sun climbs the morning sky.
Wringing wet with humidity, the beginning day dawns.
The cool, damp moments prior to sunrise are gone;
lush green grass heavy with droplets of water,
the morning wetness,
now only a waking memory
giving way to
the sweltering simmering steamy scorcher
of a sunlit day.

When you're in a hole, stop digging.

Prologue

Reagan was President and Lambert McChesney, like many kids his age, knew the threat of nuclear war and the proverbial doomsday scenario that hung over his head. With imminent death just a push of a button away, the risk of being chased by the police didn't seem all that frightening for an adolescent boy. In fact, it was something to be desired, especially being chased by the Preston Point Police, or, as the boys called them, the Pee-Pee PD.

Yet even more ominous than being chased by the cops was the thought of walking across the alleged haunted railroad bridge in the middle of the night.

Lambert was embarking upon the uncharted course of adolescence when he lived through these experiences.

Those were the days when Reagan was king and God was in his heaven and all was well with the world.

So it seemed and so he believed.

John William McMullen

The comedy of man survives the tragedy of man.
- G.K. Chesterton

THE NEIGHBORHOOD & THE BOARDING HOUSE

The neighborhood had a certain smell, feel, taste, sight, and sound. There was the donut shop, and the irresistible aroma of doughnuts and pastries wafting though the air; the corner grocery, and the sight of its regular customers; the Sinclair full service gas station with its trademark sign with the green dinosaur logo, pungent odor of gasoline, clanging service bell, dinging gas pumps, and blue and grey uniformed men washing windshields, popping hoods, and checking oil; the burger joint, and its smell of grilling meat and fried potatoes; the *Pancake Palace* and smell of bacon and eggs and freshly brewed coffee; three neighborhood bars with daily swaggerers and a pharmacy all at the intersection of Depot and Hickory; the Catholic, Lutheran, and Methodist churches and their bell towers all within denominational earshot; and the public library, police station, courthouse, jail, firehouse, bus station, and Union Depot all within a few city blocks. Three passenger trains still stopped at Preston Point in the late 1960s, but by 1973 passenger service came to an end.

Merle and Mabel Weaver, Lambert's next door neighbors, ran a boarding house, one of the last in town. The Weavers were in their seventies and their house smelled like old people. They also had a huge cockroach problem – both in quantity and size. The Weavers rented their seven upstairs rooms out, but they only rented the rooms to men, and a homemade cardboard sign hung on one of the porch pillars: *Male Roomers Only*. The boarding house had a large front porch with a swing and several chairs. Mr. Weaver and the roomers who lived upstairs would sit on the front porch at all hours of the day and night, drink beer and whiskey, chew tobacco, smoke cigarettes and cigars, talk loudly, and brag and argue about whatever men brag and argue about. Even when they were quietly sitting on the porch one could smell the liquor and tobacco and see the red glow at the end of their cigarettes.

Merle Weaver was a towering six-foot-six, broad shouldered man with about two days growth of a beard any given day. His face was fiercely strong: a large reddish nose, only four front teeth, and a protruding jaw. Merle was bald except for the sides of his head and he kept his hair cut short above his ears. He wore a baseball cap, red flannel shirt, blue bib overalls, black work boots, with white thermal long underwear showing at the neck and over his wrists. Just inside the front door of his house he kept a loaded double-barreled shotgun propped against the wall.

Merle would sit and swear, and tell old stories of his railroading days, all the while whittling wood with a large hunting knife. It was more like a dagger. He told Lambert and his brother Charles Patrick — better known as Chip — that he'd lost count of how many men he'd killed in his day: knivings, gunfights, or with his bare hands. "I done killed more men than you can shake a stick at." And even though Merle scared the hell out of Lambert and his brother Chip, the front porch beckoned the boys like a black hole draws light.

Mabel Weaver was a heavy woman and in poor health; her eyeglasses were as thick as magnifying lenses, her hearing aids were as big as her ears, and her breathing was one long laborious gasp in and wheezing hiss out. She seemingly hadn't shaved her armpits since the 1960s, and her hands and feet were freakishly withered with arthritis. Occasionally when she'd let Lambert and Chip in for a visit, Merle would just stare at them when they'd step into his living room. The boys would keep their eyes on him to make sure he didn't go for his shotgun.

Of the male roomers living at the boarding house, they were colorful, intriguing and odd, to say the least. This particular summer among the residents of the boarding house were Cecil Gordon, a black railroad conductor; Sonny Sage, a pathetically pigeon-toed, hook nosed, five-feet tall man with *Tourette's Syndrome* whose facial expressions, bodily movements, incomprehensible grunts and verbal barrages terrified the unsuspecting; Raymond Wilson, a veteran of the Vietnam War with unpredictable mood swings and explosions of profanities and obscenities; and Larry Brown, a limping brakeman with the local B & O railroad yard crew.

John William McMullen

Common sense is not so common.
 – Voltaire

John William McMullen

THE SINISTER PLOT

Wiffle Ball was a passion for Lambert and Chip and the neighborhood was their ball diamond. Directly across the alley, behind their house, was Mrs. Harrison, a recent widow. Her driveway served as the outfield to their ball diamond and anything over her fence in left field was a homerun. First base was her trash pit, second base the gate to her yard, third base the Weavers' trash pit; pitcher's mound was in the middle of the alley and home plate was the edge of the McChesneys' concrete patio.

Mrs. Harrison had gotten upset with Lambert and Chip on several occasions for playing ball too close to her tomato plants. Of course it wasn't their fault that she had planted the things in right field. Besides, Lambert thought they had only tapped the plastic ball near them a few times. One day Mrs. Harrison actually came out of her house and stood guard over the tomato plants as they played. So the boys were extra careful around her precious plants. It wasn't like they were going to hurt them; the plants never had any tomatoes on them.

On this particular day Lambert hit the ball over her trash pit and the ball lodged under one of her tomato plants.

"Oh, no!" Chip exclaimed, his hands on his head.

Lambert moaned, but tried to remain inconspicuous and didn't dare stare in that direction. Chip turned towards Mrs. Harrison's back door.

"Is she looking?" Lambert asked in a loud whisper as he jogged to her trash pit which served as first base.

"I don't see her," he replied, turning to look.

Lambert went around the side of her house and sneaked into her yard. Hurrying past her house, he crawled through the Tiger Lilies and reached for the scuffed-up ball, grey from constant use. But just as he was about to grasp the ball, his eyes spotted a nearly ripe tomato; bright orange and red, the fruit was nestled safely under the shelter of the leaves of its plant.

He paused for a moment and saw all sorts of tiny tomatoes, many of them still small and green, dotting the staked plants. Lambert knew his grandma had tomato plants and loved to grow them, and he could have them for the asking, but these were different; these belonged to a neighbor.

Lambert quickly looked for more, bigger, and riper ones.

"C'mon, Lambert! Get the ball!" Chip strained his voice in a hushed scream, "Quick! Grab the ball and go! I see her! She's in her kitchen!"

Snatching the ball, Lambert jumped up and ran back towards his house, hollering out, "I got it!"

He hurried over to Chip and explained that there really were tomatoes growing in right field. Chip didn't care. And even though Lambert resumed his play that afternoon, an idea kept recurring about those tomatoes, a wonderfully wicked idea; he couldn't seem to get it out of his head. He was definitely near the occasion of sin, experiencing a severe temptation, yet he was making plans for Mrs. Harrison's tomatoes.

Time passed and he forgot about her tomatoes until the Fourth of July weekend. He and Chip were well into their summer vacation and Mrs. Harrison was still out on tomato patrol. Lambert and Chip were still engaged in their backyard ball marathon when the sinister thoughts of tomatoes tempted Lambert once again. Mrs. Harrison came out to her car, got in, waved, and drove down the alley. It was a routine ritual for her. That's when Lambert looked around and checked the alley for witnesses.

"Lambert?" Chip asked. "What's going on?"

Lambert put his right hand to his face and raised his index finger in front of his mouth. He then looked up at the roomers' windows to make sure that no one was looking. Chip ran over to where he was standing in the middle of the alley. Some of the tomatoes were starting to ripen and getting big enough to pick, but Lambert didn't want to pick them because they were particularly large, or particularly succulent, or particularly beautiful for that matter. Nor did he need the tomatoes because he was in need of nutrition, for he didn't even like tomatoes. Neither did he have plans to steal them from the rich neighbor to give to the poor. To be quite honest it was simply a temptation to pick a tomato because it wasn't his!

Now all he really needed was an accomplice. He looked into Chip's clear blue eyes and smiled wide. A craving to possess that which belongs to another infected Lambert's soul, but he couldn't do this dastardly deed of darkness all alone. How could he alone have all that guilt on his soul? He figured he should share it with someone else, namely his brother.

Chip glared back at him. "What?"

Lambert glanced around again for possible witnesses, grabbed the plastic bat and prepared to swing. "Just pitch me the ball!" When he did so, he intentionally hit the ball over the trash cans into Mrs. Harrison's tomato plants, right in the middle of the vines. As the ball landed near the staked plants, he cried out, "I'll get it." He hustled past first base, leapt over a trash can, tumbled down, and strategically snapped off a half-ripened tomato close to the ball. He carefully hid the tomato in his left hand as he feigned surprise by grabbing the ball with his right hand, raising it up high, and exclaiming, "Here it is! I found the ball, Chip!"

He had the tomato, too. He ran over to Chip and showed it to him.

"No! You didn't?!" Chip asked disbelievingly. "What're you going to do with it, eat it?"

"No," Lambert answered, "I don't even like tomatoes. But we could watch for cars coming down Bonaventure."

"Why?"

"So we can throw the tomato at it!"

"You mean so *you* can throw a tomato." Chip was scared and

excited at the same time. He forgot about the ball game and began intently watching for cars. "Car!" He yelled out. "Okay... Now! Throw it!"

From the middle of the alley, Lambert heaved the tomato up and over his house and hoped it would hit a car. As he watched between the houses he saw the car speed by and watched the tomato hit the street, splatter, and roll to the opposite curb. He and Chip both sighed out loud.

Immediately they heard their mother open the back door and call out, "Boys! Supper's almost ready! Come in and help me set the table."

That was close. Chip and Lambert kept their misdeed to themselves. They'd accidentally hit cars with baseballs, kick balls, and plastic balls before, but never had it ever entered their heads to actually throw objects at passing cars. Yet once the idea had popped into Lambert's head it wouldn't go away until he tried it. And once he had tried it, he had to do it again.

* * * * *

Within the next few weeks Chip and Lambert had gotten into the habit of plucking a tomato here and there, and throwing them at cars. Of course they were wily enough to only do so when Mrs. Harrison's car wasn't in her driveway, knowing that she wasn't home. They were getting pretty good at lobbing tomatoes over the house, taking aim and throwing them like fastballs. Either way, it was a terrifically scary feeling when they saw the tomato hit the car on the hood, or the roof, or the trunk, but the best were windshield shots when the tomato splashed all over the front window. They'd hear the car's brakes lock up and the tires skid and squeal. Then they'd run and hide under some bushes or under a car.

One afternoon Mrs. Harrison came out of her house while the boys were playing ball. By now Lambert could barely stand to look in her direction, let alone speak with her. He figured that sooner or later she was going to notice her tomatoes disappearing; especially the ones that she was watching grow and ripen.

The moment she walked out of her back door Lambert told Chip that their mom was calling them. Of course it was a lie, but it was a ruse to get out of Mrs. Harrison's line of sight. They ran into the house and ran through the dining room and down to the hallway to their bedroom where they watched her from their window.

She walked over to the tomato plants, leaned over, reached down, and looked around. She sprang up with a frown and said, "Damn it!" She looked straight at their house.

"Oh, God," Lambert blurted out. It was a fine time to pray, but a little late.

"God doesn't have anything to do with it, Lambert!" Chip fired back.

"You did it, yourself! It was all *your* idea. You started it! She knows, man. She knows it was you. You're dead."

"*Me!* What about you?" Lambert demanded, "Where have you been, buddy?! You helped—"

"Shhh! Dummy! She'll hear you!" Chip warned.

"It doesn't matter. She knows it's us. We're dead," Lambert pondered aloud, "We're dead."

They stood lifeless as they stared out the windows, their eyes riveted on Mrs. Harrison as she stormed past her plants and marched back into her home.

"That was close," Lambert said. "I thought she was going to come over here."

"She probably will, dummy," Chip snipped. He lay down on his bed and said, "I'm sick Lammie. She's going to talk to mom and dad and we're going to be grounded for life!"

Lambert nervously fidgeted around in the bedroom and pulled open the top drawer of his dresser. He saw Mrs.

Harrison again, but this time she was walking through her backyard towards the alley. Lambert motioned for Chip to look out the window. Chip jerked in his bed with anguish in his eyes.

"There she is!" Lambert stuttered out in a half-whispery voice, "Mrs. Harrison's coming over here."

Chip shot straight up in bed and stood on top of the mattress, looking out through the linen curtains, "I'm leaving-"

"Hang on," Lambert interrupted and tried to sound encouraging, "Maybe she's just going to check her trash or something."

"Yeah, right," Chip shot back sarcastically, "You don't check your trash cans like you do the mail, moron. Admit it, Lambert. We're goners!"

At that Lambert's heart sank even lower. He eyed her again, this time walking through their back yard and crossing the improvised ball diamond.

As she stepped over home plate she had a scowl look on her face that would have taken rust off a bumper. Chip jumped under the covers and put a pillow over his head. Mrs. Harrison's face passed by their bedroom window and Lambert waited for the doorbell to ring, or, more appropriately, their death knell.

As Lambert waited for the doorbell to ring it was like waiting for a bomb to explode. When it did ring it echoed through the hallway and neither one of the boys dared go to the door.

"Why'd you steal so many of them, dumbhead!" Chip whispered loudly.

Lambert didn't answer, alone with his sin.

The doorbell rang again and Lambert heard Mrs. Harrison clear her throat as she waited for someone to answer the door. Chip and Lambert didn't move a muscle.

"Boys?" Mrs. McChesney called out. Lambert and Chip ignored her.

"Act like you're taking a nap, Chip," Lambert said while darting under his bed covers.

"Chip? Lambert? Charlie? Lambert?" Their mother got no response. "I'll get it. Where are those boys?" she said aloud as she made her way to the back door.

By now Lambert figured that Mrs. Harrison was becoming impatient. He heard her sigh and shift her feet as she waited. She was upset and really wanted to talk to someone, or else she would have just left after the second ring. No, he knew what she wanted. She wanted the tomato thieves. And she knew where she could probably find them and she probably had a pretty good idea of who they were: two young boys who looked a whole lot like Chip and Lambert, who evidently had too much time on their hands, and had nothing better to do but steal tomatoes from a poor widow.

Listening as their mom unlocked the back door, Lambert and Chip were completely still and strained to hear every word of the ensuing conversation.

Their mom pushed open the screen door and asked, "Yes, Lois?"

"Brenda?"

"How are you?"

"Not good, Brenda. I think we've got a problem."

"Son of a!" Lambert breathed out, "Okay—here it comes— brace yourself, Chip."

"Shut up!" Chip snapped, "Listen!!"

"What kind of problem, Lois?" Mother's voice resumed politely, "What happened?"

"Well, someone's been stealing my tomatoes."

"In your backyard?" Mother asked, quite surprised.

"Yes. I'm pretty upset over it. Are your boys home?"

Lambert prayed his mom would say no.

"I think so, but what do Lambert and Charlie have to do with your tomatoes?"

No, no, Lambert begged, *don't even think it, mom.* He closed his eyes, covered himself in the blanket and breathed into his pillow.

"I just want to talk to them," Mrs. Harrison continued.

"Okay. just a minute. Let me get them," she promised, not even hinting that they might not be home. Lambert prepared himself for a royal interrogation. His dad would soon be home to begin the beatings.

But in the meantime, Chip and Lambert got into character and acted like they were sleeping.

Their mother walked into their bedroom, saying, "Boys, wake up! Mrs. Harrison needs to talk to you both."

They both acted as if just rousing from an afternoon nap.

"Huh . . . uh . . . huh, wha?" Lambert began. "Who? Mom? Did'ja say something?"

"Huh?" Chip stretched. "Who's here?"

"Lois Harrison's at the back door and needs to talk to both of you boys!" she repeated herself. "Did either one of you boys steal some of her tomatoes?" she asked, not avoiding the subject at all.

"What?" Lambert swallowed nervously as he put on his best ignorant face. "I don't even like tomatoes, mom."

"Huh?" Chip said as he squinted in the light.

"Well somebody's been stealing her tomatoes from her yard. Get on out there and talk to her," she persisted.

Oh, Yeah, mom, Lambert thought. *Like I really want hurry out to face my executioner upon the scaffold. Mom, will you accompany me to the guillotine?*

Moving through the house towards the back door with Chip meekly following, Lambert asked himself how he should act. *What will I say to her?*

What is she going to ask us? What will we say? He had no answers. Perhaps he would have to tell the truth.

Lambert was the first out the door and began with small talk,

"Hi, Mrs. Harrison, How are you?" He was polite, but his speech probably revealed an intensely nervous adolescent boy.

"Well, not too well. I came over to ask if you boys knew who might be picking my tomatoes off my vines."

This was too incredible, Lambert thought. She wasn't accusing him or Chip of doing it. In fact, it almost seemed too good to be true.

"What?!" Lambert quickly retorted like he was taken totally by surprise.

"Somebody's picking your tomatoes?" Chip looked at Lambert as if waiting for his lines.

"You know who's doing it?" Chip asked with a worried tone and a guilty look, more of a statement than a question.

"If she knew, she wouldn't be asking us, right?" Lambert redirected Mrs. Harrison's attention back to himself.

"Yes, well, you two boys are outside a lot and play ball near my tomato plants," Mrs. Harrison explained further, "and I was just wondering whether you might have seen some neighborhood kids messing with them or stealing the tomatoes. Mrs. Weaver told me she found two smashed tomatoes on her front curb this morning, too. So I didn't know if you'd seen anything suspicious yesterday or last night."

Lambert couldn't speak for most liars, but he felt bad about lying, and he knew the precept *Thou shall not bear false witness against thy neighbor,* nevertheless he just couldn't tell her the truth. It would ruin her image of him and his brother Chip. And how could they have betrayed her, especially since Mr. Harrison hadn't even been dead a year, *God rest his soul*. In a split second he had it.

"Who are these kids? You just wait, Mrs. Harrison, Charlie and I will find these kids. Wait till I get my hands on them. Steal your tomatoes, will they? They won't know what hit them when we catch them, will they, Chip?!"

"Yeah, we'll find them for you, Mrs. Harrison," Chip added

to the act, "even if it means we have to stay up all night to catch 'em—"

"Oh, I think it's been happening during the day as well as the night," she disturbingly interrupted Chip as if she was on to their game. Lambert and Chip were both suddenly silent. Neither of them could bring themselves to look her in the eyes. Just then their mother stepped out and broke the muted air.

"Lois, if you need any help you just call Paul or me and we'll be right over," Mrs. McChesney said.

"Oh, thank you, Brenda, you've all been so good to me. And thank you, boys. We'll be watching for those tomato thieves. Won't we?"

"Yes," Lambert said with a brief hesitation. "Yes, we will, Mrs. Harrison. Don't you worry," he continued, regaining some confidence in his deception.

"Take care, Brenda," she said as she glanced at Lambert and Chip. "Take care of these boys of yours."

"I sure will, Lois. Thanks, bye," Mrs. McChesney waved.

"Bye, now," Mrs. Harrison said as she turned and walked back towards her house.

Lambert and Chip watched Lois Harrison make her way across the alley and back to her house.

"Boys," their mother interrupted their thoughts, "you haven't been bothering her tomato plants, have you?"

They immediately looked at each other with blank stares. "Have you?!" she asked again.

"No! We just hit our ball near them a couple of times," Lambert answered without making eye contact with his mother.

"Is that true, Charlie?"

"Uh, yeah. Yes," Chip stammered.

"You'd both better be telling me the truth because if I ever find out that you're lying and you're responsible for stealing any of her tomatoes, you know what'll happen! I'll call your Dad home from work!"

How many times had they heard threats like this before, but this time they were concerned. Lambert and Chip went back inside the house and went to their room, closed the door, and collapsed on their beds. They could breathe again; they had a new lease on life.

"Man, I'm not going to steal any more tomatoes," Lambert vowed in a whisper.

"Me either," Chip rejoined.

"Do you know how close that was?" Lambert asked.

"Too close!" Chip answered, "But what if Mrs. Harrison really knows it's us?"

"Don't think about it, Chip! You worry too much."

For the rest of that day both boys counted their blessings. Mrs. Harrison counted her tomatoes.

* * * * *

Two weeks passed and again Lambert and Chip were outside playing. Lambert was pitching the ball when Chip hit it in Mrs. Harrison's tomato patch.

"Aw, no, not again!" Lambert cried aloud. He turned and remembered that Mrs. Harrison's car wasn't there—and hadn't been there in two days. Suddenly the temptation grew with each step closer to the vines. *Thou shall not covet thy neighbor's goods*, and *Thou shall not steal*, came to mind, but they were of no use. He looked around suspiciously and bent down to get the ball. *Just one more, for old time's sake.* It was beautiful, big, red, and round and it would surely make a great projectile.

"No, Lambert! Don't!" Chip hollered out. "Just get the ball and pitch it to me!"

Lambert stood up, hiding the tomato in his left hand as he motioned with his right forefinger to his lips for Chip to shut up.

Chip started to walk towards Lambert when he heard a car.

Chip yelled "Car," as if an automatic response had gone off inside him. Lambert stood still by Mrs. Harrison's trash cans as the car drove by them in the alley. It was just one of the hippies from the other end of the alley. As he drove by he was smoking what Lambert presumed was a cigarette; a song by *The Doors* was playing full blast on the car stereo. The hippie driver cruised by without even noticing Lambert and Chip standing by the trash pit.

"Don't pick anymore of her tomatoes, stupid!" Chip said emphatically.

"I'm not going to get grounded for the rest of my summer and I'm not going to jail for stealing. Just go put it back underneath one of the plants. That way she'll think it just fell off. If you don't, I'm telling Mom."

"There you go again," Lambert interrupted, referring to the proverbial well-worn phrase: *I'm telling mom.* "Mama's boy! Well, go ahead, but I'll tell her you lied to Mrs. Harrison, and then I'll tell how you helped steal some of the tomatoes so we could throw them at cars."

Chip grunted at him.

Lambert took note that that hippie had shut off his car's engine and had gone in his house. The neighborhood was quiet. No one was looking. "Tell me when you see a car coming down Bonaventure," Lambert said as he eyed Chip.

"NO!" Chip argued. "I'm not going to do it! I'm tired of having to hide when there's still sunlight. I just want to play ball! Now c'mon and just play!

"Aw shut up!" Lambert balked.

"No, you shut up! Where's the ball?"

Lambert heard the sound of a car whistling down the street. He felt lucky; his posture betrayed his intentions.

Chip broke his concentration for just a second and yelled, "NO! Don't try it! Don't!"

From the alley Lambert saw the front bumper of the

oncoming car about a half a block away and got ready. He took the ripened, juicy tomato in his right hand and bounced on his feet, getting a good pivot point, reared back his arm and loosened up as if about to throw a baseball from centerfield to home plate. At the next glimpse of the car between the Weaver's and the next house, he delivered an overarching toss, flinging the fruit up and over.

As he released the garden tomato from his hand—just as it left his fingertips—he saw the car—two large white numerals against a black front fender. Lambert's arm was already at the two o'clock position, with the tomato rapidly climbing the cloudy sky. It was then that he realized his intended target was a police cruiser! He could not retract the catapulted tomato. It had been well thrown.

At first he thought he was imagining things, but it was no mirage. It was reality. He had done it and he couldn't take it back or prevent what would happen next. Of course, all of these thoughts flashed through his mind in less than a second in a slow-motion mind game.

"COP!" Chip yelled and glared at Lambert, "You're going to hit a cop car!" He began to make a break for it.

Lambert prayed that it would miss. He used to pray—even though it was wrong to do so—but he'd pray to hit cars. But not this time, *Oh please, God, not this one*. He dropped down on one knee, put his hands on his head and watched in horror. The trajectory appeared perfect as the tomato sank toward the moving target. The tomato sailed down, falling out of the sky like a bomb, as the squad car moved directly into ground zero.

Not only was this tomato going to be a direct hit, but the police officer had his driver's side window down. And this just wasn't a hood shot, or a trunk shot, or even a roof shot. No, it was even worse than a windshield shot. It was a *driver's side window shot*, and a head shot at that, the boldest kind of shot. And this cop got it in the left side of his cheek, right in the kisser. *Not good.*

Lambert couldn't believe it. This was worse than anything he'd ever done wrong, except, for maybe last summer when he broke Chip's foot.

He felt like he'd been shot, but he was still alive. He wanted to throw up, disappear, or die, or something, anything but be held responsible for this.

The tires of the police car skidded and squealed on the pavement in front of their house. A siren began to yelp. Poor Chip. He was running down the alley. Lambert yelled, "Chip, hide in Mrs. Harrison's yard!"

They both dove under her hedges opposite the tomato patch. Lambert's chest hurt and his heart was beating so fast and so loudly that it felt like it was in his throat. He suddenly had the urge to urinate as well.

Then the siren stopped.

"If we get out of this one," Chip whispered to Lambert, "you're dead . . . and if we get caught, I'm going to kill you."

From the way he said it Lambert didn't doubt it and he admitted that he probably deserved it. He was damned if he did and damned if he didn't.

For a second he thought he would prefer being killed by his dad rather than by his brother. Chip would likely torture him first then kill him just to let him know that he'd suffered before he died. But Lambert opted for life. Besides, his dad had never come through with any of his death threats. Yet, that is. Lambert thought the death threats were mainly used for effect, but nothing like this had happened before.

Just then he heard a car coming up the alley and it was moving slowly, the kind of slow where someone's looking for somebody. The black and white police car, car twenty-two, was feet away, and the police officer was searching for the perpetrator of the crime. All the while the cop was wiping tomato from his face with a handkerchief.

Lambert prayed the cop would keep on going. To his surprise, he did. However, Lambert and Chip waited for ten minutes before leaving their makeshift foxhole, making sure the cop never came back through the alley.

Finally, just when they thought they were given the all clear, they heard a screen door being opened. It wasn't the Weavers' door and it wasn't the hippies' door. No, it was none other than Mrs. Harrison's door. Lambert looked back out from under the hedges, and it was her!

How can that be? He asked himself with great fear. *Her car is gone. She isn't supposed to be home. She must have seen me pick the tomato.*

She went over to her water hose, turned it on, and dragged it over to her tomato plants and began watering them. While she had the water running, Chip and Lambert looked at each other and without saying a word they crawled out of the hedges and made it to the end of the block.

Lambert prayed they weren't seen. Together they ran around the block to their house and went in the front door. Lambert suggested that it would be best to go back outside again and act like they were just coming out for the first time that day to play ball. As they got outside Lambert grabbed the ball bat and prepared himself in the batter's box as he called out to Chip. "Pitch me the ball. Come on, pitch it!"

"I don't have it, "Chip said, "Don't you have it?"

"No . . . Where is it?" But then Lambert remembered where it was. In his madness of picking the tomato he forgot to get it out of the tomato vines after Chip had hit it there. He glanced over and Mrs. Harrison was examining her tomatoes as she sprinkled them with water.

"Hi, boys!" Mrs. Harrison said, as if she had just noticed them. Lambert acted like he didn't see her until then. "Oh, hello, Mrs. Harrison. How are you?"

"Pretty good, though I've been without a car for about two

days."

"Yeah. We noticed it was gone," Chip said without thinking.

"Maybe those kids will come around tonight if they think I'm gone, huh?" she said, adjusting the hose's nozzle.

"What's that?" Lambert played dumb.

"You know. The tomato thieves," she answered looking right at him as if she had known it was him all the time.

"Where's your car?" Lambert changed the subject back to her car.

"My son took it in to the shop for some repairs and an oil change," she said.

"Oh, I hope it doesn't cost you too much," he said in a concerned tone.

"Yes. Some of those places can rob you blind."

Guilt rotted his stomach and his bowels nearly moved.

"Say . . ." she hesitated and turned the nozzle off. "Lambert, come here a second...."

"Sure," he said. What else could he say? He was supposed to be the good kid next door, her friend, her ally, her defender against the tyranny of the terrible tomato thieves. He made his way over to the fence.

"Look there," she said, pointing to the scuffed-up plastic white ball under her tomato plants, "I think I found your ball."

"Oh, well, uh . . ." he faltered.

"But you know, I could've sworn that there was a tomato there about the same size as that plastic ball just last night . . ." Mrs. Harrison said while they both stood staring at the ball on the ground. She bent down and grabbed it. Turning towards Lambert, she raised and looked him in the eye. "Strange, isn't it?" She then handed him the ball with a slight smirk on her face.

"Thanks," he said, taking the ball from her hand. Briefly her fingers grazed his.

"You're welcome," she replied.

Lambert returned to play more balls, but somehow his heart

just wasn't in it anymore that day. He and Chip played for only about ten more minutes and then they went in.

On Saturday afternoon he and Chip were both in line for confession at St. Joseph's Parish.

If we pray "Our Father" we must acknowledge that He is the common Father of us all.
- Saint Ambrose

JIMMY

One of the neighborhood boys was Jimmy Wilderman. Jimmy was a year younger than Lambert and a year older than Chip.

His father, Carl Wilderman, wasn't very friendly and was suspicious of Lambert's family, particularly of their religious faith: *Catholicism*. Carl lived at the other end of the alley. Just about everybody called Carl, "Old Man Wilderman." Even Jimmy called his dad, "Old Man." (If Lambert had called his dad "Old Man," he'd been a dead man).

Old Man Carl Wilderman was about 50 years old and Jimmy was an only child. Carl drove a pick-up truck; his shotgun hung in its back window. That bothered Lambert and Chip's mother. "He's trying to find himself," she told them. On his back bumper were two stickers. One read: *I don't brake for Iranians*; the other read: *I'm for Gun Control — Hit Your Target*.

"You start lugging a gun around, a guy's liable to use it sooner or later," Mr. McChesney told his sons one night when he saw Carl drive by.

Carl rarely took Jimmy to church, but according to him all Catholics were going to hell. But Carl was very pleased that he was on the moral up n' up since he didn't drink. Not a drop of "the devil's brew" had ever tainted his lips and his soul was "pure and free of the evil of alcohol." At least that's the way he put it.

Elizabeth Wilderman, Jimmy's mother, was a Catholic but Carl never allowed her to go to Church. When she came down with cancer it left her bedridden. She died in spring of 1980. Jimmy was only twelve years old when she died.

At the time Lambert really didn't know how to deal with him losing his mother. Lambert avoided the subject thinking that if he were to dwell upon it, his own mother might get sick and die. But even while his mother was dying of cancer Jimmy and his dad sort of ignored the fact, or, to Lambert, it seemed that they were ignoring the fact that she was dying. When she died Jimmy called Lambert. "My mom's gone. She died tonight."

Lambert remembered her funeral. Jimmy sat in a chair and stared out the window of the funeral home. His dad was up and around talking all the time, making it seem that were he to be quiet for any amount of time then he would have had to face the reality of the death of his wife.

Jimmy looked up to Lambert and Chip's mom from then on. In fact, since Jimmy no longer had a mother, in a way Mrs. McChesney became his mom; she was a mother to a lot of lost boys in their neighborhood. Jimmy would sometimes eat lunch or dinner with the McChesneys – or both. Jimmy was intrigued by their Catholic faith and puzzled with some of it, too, for instance, the reverence for Mary and the saints.

"All Catholics have a Mother," Lambert told him. Granted, he and Chip had a mother and two grandmothers, but they also had the Blessed Mother, Mary. "Since Mary is the Mother of Jesus, and Jesus is our brother, then His Mother must also be our Mother. Our pastor told us that Jesus gave us his Mother so we would always have a mother no matter what happened to our earthly mothers." It didn't mean much to Jimmy.

One evening Carl Wilderman pulled up in front of Lambert and Chip's house, got out of his truck and hollered at them, "Hey, you boys seen Jimmy?"

"No," Lambert answered.

Just then Mr. Wilderman turned and saw Sonny Sage sitting on the Weavers' front porch. Sonny Sage was the hook-nosed roomer with *Tourette's Syndrome.*

"Aw, hell! There's that damned pigeon-toed freak!" Carl shouted. "Drunker than hell all the time, jumping in and out of traffic! He's a scourge to the neighborhood! They should've locked him up in the insane asylum years ago! Hell, I wouldn't be surprised if he's a murderer – kills little kids and eats them. I wouldn't be a bit surprised if he eats dogs and cats!

"Just look at him! Swatting and a swearing, 'batcrap this' and 'catturd that!' I look for him to burn down the boarding house one night! You ever see that weirdo out playing in the trash pits in the alley? Starting fires here and there, setting fire to anything he can get his hands on! Hell, I seen him set his own jacket on fire and he stood there clapping and cheering as it was burning. What a dumb-ass! He's a real freak, I'm telling you. I told Jimmy that if he ever gets near him to run like hell and come get me! My shotgun will knock some sense in the silly bastard!"

Old Man Wilderman rambled on as Mrs. McChesney opened the front door and came out onto her porch. "Could you lower your voice and watch your language, Carl," she interrupted Mr. Wilderman's running monologue, looking hard at him. "Sonny does have some problems, but must you remind the man? He *can* hear, you know. He probably heard every word you said – I know my boys did."

Mr. Wilderman shook his head, gave a smirk, and a chuckle, "Hoity-toity, I don't give a good goddamn..."

At that Old Man Wilderman got back in his truck, gunned his engine and drove off. Mrs. McChesney shook her head and went back in the house. Lambert stood on the porch and saw Sonny sitting, smoking a cigarette, staring off in the distance. Lambert knew there was a good side to Sonny, but for men like Old Man Wilderman a bullet was the answer to just about any problem.

Lambert had a feeling there was a reason Sonny Sage moved in next door. Lambert wasn't free from blame in poking fun at Sonny though. In fact, all of the boys had taken turns heckling him, but he had never hurt anyone.

The most vivid memory of Old Man Carl Wilderman was

last Halloween. Two houses down from the Wilderman's lived several foreign students. Unfortunately, in 1981, due to the hostage crisis in Iran, the attitude of the country was against foreigners – Iranians in particular. But in reality anyone who looked Middle-Eastern was fair game.

As a Halloween prank, Jimmy Wilderman soaped the car windows of the foreign students – and lit some firecrackers on their porch. Chip and Lambert heard the explosions and turned around in time to see Jimmy jumping over the hedge only to trip and fall in the street.

Two of the foreign students jumped over the hedge, screaming out, "You! Stop you! Come back here!" They were like giants compared to Jimmy and easily caught up to him as he hobbled to his feet in the middle of the street. They grabbed Jimmy by the collar of his jacket and dragged him back to the curb as he kicked and screamed for his dad. Jimmy looked at Lambert and Chip with terrified eyes as the foreign guys carried him back into their yard. "Hurry, guys! Help! Go get my Dad! Quick!!!" Jimmy squawked as he tried to squirm free.

The boys ran to tell Old Man Wilderman. Chip knocked on his door. It seemed like he'd never answer. When Carl appeared at the door he was wearing only a green bath towel around his waist and was drying his hair with a smaller white towel, "Yeah, what do *you two* want? Jimmy's not here."

"Carl, those foreign guys have got Jimmy!" Chip exclaimed.

"Jimmy lit firecrackers on their porch!" Lambert said, unsure if he should have.

Carl swung his door open and came tromping out to the end of his porch, barefooted, bare-chested, and dripping wet. He couldn't see Jimmy from where he was standing, but they could all hear him yelling for his dad.

An Arabic foreign voice sounded, "You, boy – you no leave here! No leave until windows clean. You clean windows! What you put on them?"

Another distinct foreign voice began, "You – look at me – you going to clean those windows off. You did this. You cannot do that. You ruined our windows. You stay here! And what was that you shot off?? You let fire bomb off –"

"Jimmy!" Old Man Wilderman shouted. "Where are you, Jimmy?"

"I'm over here, Dad!" Jimmy whined. "Help me! Help me! They're going to kill me, Dad!"

In his bath towel and bare feet, Carl jumped off his porch and tromped down the sidewalk in front of the foreign students' house. With Lambert and Chip close behind, Carl yelled out to them, "Hey! You, freakin' bastards, leave my boy alone! Let him go, or I'll make you wish you never came to America!" The two men came into view holding Jimmy as they looked at the freshly soaped windows on their Trans Am.

"No! He cleaning our windows," a voice returned, "He put something on them, now him going to clean windows—"

"You give me my boy, you smelly bastards—he's a good boy!"

"No, he stay with us to clean our windows. Him no good boy. Now you leave! He bad. He try to bomb us with little bombs. He could have hurt us. You stay away. This our business. He stay here until he clean windows. You – you go away!"

Old Man Wilderman turned and ran back to his house, his feet pounding loudly on the concrete, "I warned you, you sonsabitches!! That's it!! This is war!"

Lambert and Chip's attention refocused on the apartment house. Jimmy was kicking and screaming as a third foreigner held Jimmy's neck, making him scrape the car windows with an old snow scraper. Everything was happening so fast, Chip started yelling, "Hey, let him go! He's just a kid!"

Then Lambert heard two loud bangs. He and Chip turned around and looked. It was Carl Wilderman. He had kicked his front screen door so hard that it swung wide open and hit the wall only to immediately slam shut. Wild with fury, he jumped off of his porch; he was wearing a tank top, blue jeans and cowboy boots – and he was carrying a double-barreled shot gun. He ran down the sidewalk to the house where Jimmy was being held.

Carl got to the front steps, cocked his gun, took aim, and hollered out, "If you don't let my boy go, I'm gonna smoke every one of you flea-bitten sand-niggers!"

One of the students grabbed Jimmy and carried him into the house.

"You no shoot!" one of the other two students shouted as they scrambled into their apartment.

"You let him go, or I'll start shooting you sonsabitches!" Carl yelled.

" No!" a voice sounded from inside the house, "You no shoot. You not right. Crazy! Crazy, man. Man you crazy! Don't shoot–"

"You shut up!" Carl fired back, "I'll do as I damn well please!"

"Don't shoot! We make boy clean windows. He almost done. You take boy home later –"

"Shut up! I'm gonna waste all you camel jockeys!" Carl raised the gun to his shoulder and put his finger on the trigger. He began cursing with scores of expletives.

Chip ducked behind a parked grey Oldsmobile and Lambert bolted for home.

Lambert ran as fast as he could back to his house and dashed down to the basement phone to dial 9-1-1—clear of his mom and dad's earshot. They didn't need to know what was unfolding. By the time Lambert called the police he was completely out of breath. When the dispatcher answered all he could say was, "Old Man Carl Wilderman's got a gun and he's going to shoot his neighbors 'cause they caught his boy soaping their windows...."

Lambert finally got the information across to the dispatcher after repeating about three times that Jimmy was being held hostage.

As he ran up the basement steps and back into the alley, he saw Cecil Gordon, one of the roomers, getting out of his old 1970s light blue Buick Electra. "Mr. Cecil, I mean Mr. Gordon. You've got to help! You've got to help us! You've got to help Jimmy, Jimmy Wilderman!"

"My, my, what is it, Lambert!" Cecil locked his car and walked toward Lambert.

"It's a long story," Lambert began, "but Jimmy soaped his foreign neighbors' windows and they were making him clean it up. Then his dad came out with a shot gun and he's threatening to shoot them because they're holding him hostage."

"Now slow down! Who's he goin' to shoot?"

"The foreign students. He's going to kill them! Maybe you can talk him out of it."

Cecil hesitated at first, but then shook his head and said, "Okay, let's go! I'll see what I can do."

Railroad conductor Cecil Gordon was a man larger than life. He kept Lambert and Chip entertained in the evenings with stories of how he had survived numerous attempts on his life from drunken and angry railroaders. As a black man, or as he still called himself, a "colored," he was a rarity on the railroad as a conductor. Many of the old timers on the railroad resented his being hired by the Louisville & Nashville. Some of the men refused to ride the cabooses with him – even adding an extra caboose to their local freight train when they could just to avoid him. On occasion his locker had been pried open with a crowbar and his possessions were strewn along the trackside.

One time Merle Weaver, who called himself the "biggest and baddest" railroader on the C & E.I., accused Cecil of cheating at cards and tossed him off the end of the caboose on a trip between Chicago and Terre Haute. Cecil survived despite the fall even though the train was moving nearly fifty miles an hour. According to Cecil, he was the only man to ever survive one of Merle's tirades. All the other men were dead. *Dead men tell no tales.* From then on Merle respected Cecil; perhaps he considered it a sign from God. Cecil knew otherwise. If he were to report Merle's behavior Merle would lose his job – and his pension, not to mention that "the NAACP would be breathing down Merle's ass quicker than you could say Jackie Robinson," Cecil said. Cecil supposed that since he had cheated death that was why Merle allowed him to rent a room from him. Or it may have been for other reasons, but Cecil wasn't sure.

Meantime Cecil and Lambert ran down to the end of the alley where they saw Carl Wilderman standing in the street, taking aim at the students' house.

Cecil called out to him, "Sir."

Carl either ignored him or didn't hear him.

Cecil called again, this time louder, "Mr. Wilderman! Put the gun down!"

Old Man Wilderman slowly pulled the gun away from his face, turned toward Cecil, arrogantly smirked, and said, "Well, well, well...What do you know, la-de-da, the highfalutin neighborhood coon! What do you want, you high and mighty nigger boy?"

Cecil didn't flinch as he stepped in Carl's direction.

"You ain't got nothing to say here, nigger!" Carl continued. "Don't you dare try and tell me what to do! You think I ought to spare them? Them A-rab bastards got my boy! Hell, you're just as bad," he said waving the barrel of the gun in Cecil's direction. "Go on. Step in my line a fire, see if I care. Makes no difference to me. I'll shoot your black ass, too!"

Cecil shook his head and took two more steps towards Old

Man Wilderman and said, "Look, Carl – it is Carl, isn't it?"

"Where in the hell do you get off calling me by my first name, boy?" Carl said as he stepped towards Cecil. "Niggers don't use my first name – or last name – boy! You understand? That don't go over here, nigger. My name's nothin' to you! Now you get your black ass away from me or I'll turn it around for you! You refer to me as Mister, unless you prefer to call me 'Master,' he said with a laugh. "Don't make me use this on your ass! Now stand back and get it out of my line of fire 'cause I'm gonna shoot me some A-rabs!"

At that instant Lambert heard a revving car engine and screeching tires. A black and white police car pulled up in the street and two officers got out, drew their weapons, and shielded themselves behind their cruiser's car doors. One of the officers told everyone to get out of the way, so Chip, Cecil, Lambert, and a few neighborhood gawkers hurried across the street. Another squad car pulled up and before long there were cops and guns everywhere. All the attention centered upon Carl.

"Step away from the car! Drop your weapon!" A megaphone emerged from a half opened door on the squad car as a male voice broke the evening air.

Carl Wilderman slowly obeyed the order.

"Put your hands in the air and spread you legs." The megaphone voice commanded as the officer rose to his feet.

The police officers then rushed upon him. Among their number were Officer Ron Spike and his police dog, Goofy.

"I'll have your badges!" Old Man Wilderman yelled at the officers as they led him to the back seat of one of the police cruisers.

Lambert and Chip lingered around until they saw one of the cops leading Jimmy out of the foreign students' apartment. Jimmy hollered from across the street, "I'm okay, guys. See you tomorrow." He waved happily as if nothing had happened.

Then Carl emerged from the squad car and one of the older, white haired cops patted him on the back, handed him back his shot gun, and said him, "Carl, just go on home and don't worry about these foreign guys. We'll take care of things."

All the cops got in their cars and drove away – except Sergeant Ron Spike and his dog Goofy. He stayed behind to interrogate the foreign students.

Spike was notorious for being a hapless cop with shiny silver sunglasses and a German shepherd in his backseat, but he was still feared nonetheless.

As Lambert and Chip made their way through the alley and headed for home, they could hear lots of yelling and shouting and barking between Spike and the young men and Goofy.

Lambert looked around for Cecil Gordon to thank him but saw no sign of him. And his blue Buick Electra was gone.

Afterwards Jimmy vowed never to mess with the foreign guys again. Old Man Wilderman vowed he would kill them if there ever was a next time.

Stupidity is also a gift of God,
but one mustn't misuse it.
- Pope John Paul II

SLUSHY SPIKE

Lambert would often find himself down at Eugene Thomas's house on the opposite end of the block. Eugene Thomas was about the same age as Lambert, but he was a much bigger kid. Eugene didn't have a dad, or at least he never talked about one. Lambert wondered if Eugene's dad was dead but none of the boys ever asked Eugene about him. Eugene's mother was always on the go and rarely home. When she was home she seemed to either be sleeping or watching television. One time Eugene explained that she worked nights but he never said where. Eugene's house was a crumbling brick house painted a gaudy orange whose paint was peeling while the brick porch sagged away from the front of the house. The lawn consisted of dandelions, crabgrass, wild onions, and bare spots.

Eugene was great at spinning tales. He told Lambert he crawled out his bedroom window onto the roof of his front porch and lying on his stomach he shot the last of his bottle-rockets from his BB-gun at oncoming cars. Of course, Lambert always wondered whether any story Eugene told was true, but he usually accepted them as fact rather than fiction.

About sunset, in the dusty, humid heat of a late August day, as the cicadae whined loudly, and the donut shop's neon sign crackled with electricity, Lambert, Chip, Jimmy made their way to Eugene's. When they saw him he was chopping one of his mother's trees with a small hatchet. He kept hacking away and laughing about it when suddenly he stopped and smiled with a glint in his eye: Larry Brown wearing his Pittsburg Pirate ball cap was walking down the sidewalk. Larry Brown was one of the roomers who lived at the Weavers' boarding house.

Eugene stood up on his picnic table and looked across the yard. "It's the grubworm!"

Larry "Grubworm" Brown moved into the boarding house in the summer of 1979. The boys called him "Grubby" because he had a perpetual five o'clock shadow and his clothes were grease stained and dirty. He always wore an old Pittsburgh Pirate baseball cap and slumped with a limp when he walked. He was a brakeman with the Baltimore & Ohio Railroad yard crew. And he was forever dangling off the end of a railroad car and one could tell it was him from a few blocks away by the way he slumped as he gripped the handrail and stood on the freight car's step.

Eugene jumped off the bench and ran three paces forward with the hatchet in his left hand. "Watch this!" he said. Eugene reared back and threw the axe in a perfect tomahawk-toss, head over handle, aiming it at one of the trees which lined the boulevard.

Larry Brown was walking right into the path of the flying axe. The hatchet soared by him, just missing his head as it lodged in the center of the trunk of the tree in front of Eugene's house. Larry jerked his head away as the axe flashed in front of his face. He stopped and looked at the axe lodged in the tree's bark. Then he turned to look at Eugene's smiling face.

He resumed walking, though hurrying along, limping slightly, walking down the sidewalk in the direction of the boarding house. Eugene ran over and pulled the hatchet from the side of the tree and hid it in his house.

Chip and Jimmy roiled in laughter so hard they could hardly stand. Lambert knew it was wrong, but part of him was so happy for Eugene since he hadn't killed Larry with a tomahawk toss. And Lambert certainly didn't want to challenge Eugene, so he laughed.

Nervously.

For the next twenty minutes the four boys sat on Eugene's porch watching the sunset of orange and purple, still giggling from time to time about Larry's reaction to the axe. As the sound of cicadae droned on, a car abruptly screeched up on the curb with a spotlight shining on them.

"Cops!" Eugene moaned, motioning for the guys to do something.

The boys were blinded like criminals frozen in the headlights of an oncoming car. Lambert heard a police radio as the officer opened his car door and got out. The door shut and the steps of the officer approached the porch. He slowly walked up the concrete steps aiming his flashlight at them. He looked up and tilted his head. It was much too late to run.

"All right – which one of you hoodlums threw that axe?" The officer demanded to know, shining his light in each of the boy's faces. Lambert couldn't see whether there was another officer with him due to the car's blinding spotlight.

"What're you talking 'bout?" Eugene said.

"Don't give me that boy – I just got a call that one of you goofballs threw a danged axe at one of the roomers from the boarding house."

The voice was that of Sergeant Ron Spike.

"Which one?" asked Eugene.

"You know damn good and well which one, young man!" Turning his glare towards the others he asked, "Now which of the four of you did it? Huh? Who threw the axe, or didn't you see anything either?" Officer Spike's police dog, Goofy, began barking from the back seat, his head hanging out the cruiser's half-opened back window on the driver's side.

Lambert didn't dare say anything. If he did, he knew that Eugene would likely kill him with his hatchet. It was good to have Eugene on your side, and Lambert wanted to stay on his good side, so he kept his mouth shut. Lambert was sure that Chip and Jimmy weren't saying anything either for exactly the same reason.

Eugene interrupted at that point and said, "They weren't even down here ten minutes ago, were you guys?"

"Uh, yeah, that's right," Lambert stammered.

"No...uh...I just got here," Chip replied like an actor who had forgotten his lines.

"I didn't see nothing, man. No axe, no guy, no nothing," Jimmy added for good measure.

"Thomasina, isn't it?" Sergeant Spike smirked and chuckled to himself, glaring at Eugene.

"***Thomas***." Eugene said forcefully before turning to spit on the sidewalk.

"Watch how you speak to me, boy. I could charge you with provocation *and* defacing public property with your snot."

Eugene said nothing as Spike stared all of them down while pacing in front of them.

"Say, aren't you that Wilderman kid?" Spike asked as he eyed Jimmy, "Didn't I save your butt once before? Yeah, last year you were the little vandal with illegal fireworks. Yeah, I remember you."

Addressing all of them he continued his interrogation, "Now listen boys, and listen good — you all better not be lying to me, or else there'll be hell to pay." He placed his right hand on the handle of his revolver and caressed the gun slightly before resuming his speech. "And just to be sure, I'm going to be watching you real close. You can count on that. Remember me. I'm Sergeant Spike. My friends call me *Hell Spike* for short. And if I hear of you causing any more trouble or if I get another call to come out here, you'll regret the day you ever messed with me!"

He walked back to his big black and white four-door Chrysler cruiser, got in, turned off the spotlight, lit up a cigarette, took a drag, blew some smoke their direction, then drove off the curb making a U-turn in the street in front of us, drove down the street, pulled up in front of the Weaver's Boarding House, and turned his headlights off.

"That was a dare if I ever heard one," Eugene said with a grin. "Hell Spike? More like Wimpy Chicken. I should have asked him if he wanted a Slushy."

It seemed everyone in town knew Officer Spike because of the incident last year near Slushy's Root Beer Stand when he had been running radar out on Second Street. He had parked his police cruiser on the curb and he was leaning against the rear of his car facing on-coming traffic with his radar gun in his hand; he was wearing mirrored sun-glasses with his head cocked back and arms crossed.

As one car passed by Spike, one of the kids inside flung a Slushy milkshake out the window. It was a bull's-eye — the slushy flew right into his crotch and splashed all over him. Many of the high school cruisers and bystanders who saw what happened howled in laughter. His face was covered with chocolate. He peeled his messy sunshades off his dripping face, wiping his face and hair with his handkerchief, as chocolate ice cream dripped down his pants. He jumped in his squad car, spun his tires in the grass till he bounced off the curb. Then he squawked his tires for half a block, white smoke pouring from them. He drove madly down the middle of the two-lane street between the cars in both lanes to catch the culprits, but he got hung up in traffic and was trapped between two cars. Not only that, but his car stopped right on top of the railroad tracks — and everybody heard the horns of an approaching train.

Spike honked, turned his red lights and siren on, rolled his window down and shouted for the people to let him through, but no one could move. They were stuck, too. A fast moving freight train came around the bend at better than forty miles an hour with the horn blaring. It was too late for the engineer to stop his train. The airbrakes locked on as sand sprayed on the rails under the engine's wheels; the train jerked and rocked as the couplers banged violently and dust and debris flew up and out from under the train.

People screamed for Spike to get out of his car. Right before the engines plowed into his police car, he bailed out of the driver's side door and rolled away from the tracks. Goofy jumped out the open door and the four engine freight train smashed his squad car to smithereens. It was stuck on the front of the train for a few seconds, crinkling up under the lead engine and scraping everything in front of it, skidding sideways, taking with it two of the automatic crossing signals before flipping away and rolling over a couple of times like a tin can. Finally the wreckage came to rest at the side of the tracks.

Witness saw a spark and a flash of light right before the car exploded in a burst of flame. A column of black smoke billowed over Slushy's Root Beer stand. People came from all directions to see what was burning. The train finally came to a standstill, but there was smoke and flames gushing out of the blackened patrol car. Officer Spike regained his composure and started directing traffic around the scene of the crash. He was dazed yet his face was red and his hair was standing on end because he'd lost his hat. All the while he was still drenched in chocolate up and down his uniform. His shirt was a gooey mess, but his pants had a large blob of melted ice cream over his groin.

The town rumor was that the Preston Point Police Department was so embarrassed over the incident that they reassigned Spike to the graveyard shift. Spike claimed he had requested the change because he was looking for a challenge. Since then he had driven a so-called unmarked car.

His unmarked car was still a black and white cop car but the roof was bald, meaning that the police car had no emergency bubble lights on top. Instead he had a small egg-shaped red bulb mounted on his dashboard. following his unfortunate debacle with that flying chocolate shake and his subsequent disaster with an B & O locomotive, the only trouble with his "unmarked car" was that it was far from a slick undercover car: a two-tone four door Chrysler luxury sedan, with five antennas springing from the trunk lid, and two large white seventy-sevens written on both sides of the front fenders. Who couldn't tell that behind the wheel of this unmarked squad car was a cop with an attitude?

Now Spike had met his match in Eugene.

Meanwhile Spike flipped his headlights on, pulled away from the curb in front of the boarding house, turned on his siren, placed his egg-shaped red light on the dash, and sped down the street, evidently responding to another call. Eugene jumped off his porch and yelled, "PIG!" just as Spike soared by.

Lambert started to dart for Eugene's porch, but Eugene grabbed him by his belt loop. "Where you going, chicken?! That cop's inviting us to stir up trouble. I'm going to get him good, and you guys are going to help." Eugene glared at Lambert, Chip, and Jimmy. "Aren't you?"

Lambert thought he had a hairball in his throat. How could he say no to Eugene Thomas, the biggest and toughest kid in the neighborhood? Lambert was in a fix and either way he knew it would cost him.

Whoever does not love a neighbor
whom he has seen
cannot love God whom he has not seen.
1 John 4:20

John William McMullen

SCOTT LAWRENCE

Beginning last summer Lambert began to observe a strange and oddly dressed bearded man around town. He noticed him seemingly everywhere. Wherever Lambert went, the bearded man was standing on a street corner, sitting in a restaurant, walking down the street, or begging someone for money.

Lambert remembered the first time he ever saw him. It was an airless August afternoon and he wasn't hard to spot because of how he was dressed. It was ninety plus degrees outside with one hundred percent humidity when he happened down the sidewalk in front of Lambert's house. The man was wearing a women's fur coat. His walk was unmistakable: his head hung as low as his shoulder blades slouched. He ambled along slowly and his head sagged as he looked at the ground. As he approached, Lambert noted that he had on two different kinds of shoes – one running shoe and the other a casual slip-on dress shoe. His hair was long and in his face. He had a mustache and a full beard that draped over the front of his coat. Lambert wondered how he could be so cold in the blazing heat.

As he passed in front of Lambert he said nothing, which was odd for Preston Point. Everybody usually nodded or waved, or in the very least grunted hello. He did none.

As summer progressed people began to talk and soon Lambert learned that his name was Scott Lawrence. He was homeless and he needed money.

The first time Lambert ever saw Scott at church was at a Sunday evening Mass. Scott was sitting on the left side of Church near the Sanctuary. Not many people, though, were sitting around him.

One family went into the pew directly behind him and knelt down, but about a minute later they shot out of the pew and moved across the aisle away from him. Lambert noticed that several people repeated the same process. They would go in and if they were anywhere near Scott moments later they would bolt out of their pew and move across the church, all the while looking at Scott with critical eyes and furrowed brow. Scott needed a bath.

Folks around town said Scott slept in a Hefty trash bag, but he was a good looking young man when he was clean shaven. Lambert wondered where he had grown up, how long he had been homeless, and why he was homeless.

All during Mass Scott never stood or knelt, but just sat with his head down. Father Clement's sermon that day, of all days, was about looking for Christ in one another, taking the time to see Jesus in one's neighbor. It made Lambert think. The Gospel story was about the rich man and the poor man, Lazarus. Lambert wondered if God had inspired Scott to come to Church that particular day.

In the parable, the poor man had been lying in the alleyway near the rich man's house for quite some time. Yet in all that time the rich man never noticed him in his need, never giving him as much as a crumb. Even the neighborhood dogs showed compassion for Lazarus. The rich man, on the other hand, wore expensive fine linen and purple garments and sat and ate at his large banquet table, consuming huge, wonderful meals every day. Lambert thought God surely had a great sense of humor, but Mr. McChesney said Scott probably knew ahead of time which Gospel passage was going to be read knowing he'd get plenty of sympathy money.

Before Communion, Scott got out of his pew and walked out of church. After Mass, as the parishioners were descending the front steps returning to their cars, Scott was at the bottom step with his hand out. Many, if not most, of the parishioners, even though probably out of guilt, Lambert supposed, were walking over, reaching into their pockets and purses or going for their wallets and stretching forth their hands dropping dimes, quarters, and dollars into his extended hand.

There was one thing that really bothered Lambert: Scott never said 'thank you'. Yet Lambert knew the rule, "Judge not, lest ye be judged." Besides, he wasn't homeless.

Scott would seek his benefactors out like a bear after honey and then try and talk about anything and everything before getting to the real purpose for the encounter. With his eyes batting and rolling around in his head, he would stutter and wring his hands, put them in his pockets and then take them out repeatedly. Then he'd wring his hands some more and look around, yet careful to never quite look the person in the eyes, and then he'd hold out his palms in the person's direction. Then he'd put his hand up to his face, stroke his beard and face, and run his long dark fingers through his thick dirty brown hair.

Once the person finally gave in – and it was hard not to, unless, of course, one actually didn't have any money, of which Scott would somehow know intuitively. He could tell whether someone was lying about not having any money and he had it down to an art. Yet once the would-be contributor finally caved in and gave him a quarter or a buck or whatever he had, he'd drop him like a hot potato and move on to his next donor.

Scott began going to different churches every Sunday, plying his trade, bumming money off of unsuspecting believers.

Lambert's dad called it panhandling.

One downtown church kicked him out during Sunday services, but that was because they didn't allow anyone who wasn't dressed properly. Cecil Gordon said that church wasn't fond of Negroes either.

It was a phenomenal thing to watch Scott Lawrence. By observing his dress any particular day, one could always tell the popular styles from ten to fifteen years before. One time

Lambert saw two human legs sticking out of a Goodwill drop-box. The legs kicked and a person eventually emerged. It was just Scott fetching himself some new clothes, avoiding the middle man.

It's no wonder why he looked like a garage sale explosion. Plaid on plaid, stripes on stripes, long-sleeve turtlenecks and high-water polyester pants with white tube socks and white buck dress shoes. T-shirts with slogans, over-sized blue jeans with the legs rolled up, old converse high-top basketball gym shoes; light blue and bright green sport coats with tight non-matching suit pants and cowboy boots, with one pants leg stuck in one boot and the other leg down.

One morning Lambert went outside and Scott eyed them in the alley. Scott was wearing a blue "I'm with stupid" t-shirt, tight yellow shorts, red socks and brown wing-tip dress shoes. Jimmy Wilderman came down the alley on his bike just as Scott began to ply his trade.

"Don't give that bum any money, Lambert!" Jimmy said.

"He's got to eat," Lambert explained.

"Heck-fire, he ain't eating. He's drinking! If you give him any money, he'll go o'er to the Purple Finch Tavern."

"He says he doesn't have a job," Lambert answered.

"My Dad says 'He wouldn't work if he had to,'" Jimmy said. "Heck, I'll bet he's been stashing all that money. He probably makes more money in an hour than your old man makes all day!"

"Jimmy, you don't know that,' Lambert countered, recalling the lesson his grandmother had always taught him about not judging others. "Besides he might be an angel in disguise—"

"Yeah, a fallen angel! Man, Lambert, I can't believe you give your money to a good for nothing bum!"

Another hot August day while Lambert was shooting hoops

with Chip and Jimmy, Scott approached them clad in a red, white, and green plaid coat and tight neon green Capri pants, and red and blue bowling shoes. He stood before them and said, "Uh, hi Jeff. Think it'll rain?" He often called people Jeff, as if an all-purpose name.

"Not really," Lambert answered, not sure who he was speaking to since he was still staring at the ground. "It's too hot!"

"Is it?" he asked, turning his face up toward the sun, but rolling his eyes around without looking at them directly.

"Are you cold, Scott?" asked Chip.

"I don't know."

"It's ninety-five degrees, man!" Jimmy exclaimed. "How can you stand that coat?"

"Well, uh, I just feel cold," he explained with a shrug of his shoulders while closing his eyes.

Lambert thought he smelled alcohol on his breath, but he didn't say anything. Lambert began to walk away trying to avoid the inevitable.

"Uh, it's a, it's a nice coat and all, uh huh," he rambled on, "warm, but, uh, you know, I'm just trying to get together enough money for a cup of coffee—"

Lambert interrupted him, "So, how's your job hunt, Scott?"

"Well, it's just not...people ain't hiring anymore, nowhere. There's no jobs anymore."

"Have you put in your application anywhere?"

"Uh...well, uh.... No. You know, they don't do those anymore—"

"They don't?!" Lambert asked. "I hadn't heard."

"I think it's because of President Reagan or something. I think he passed a law. But, uh, you know, I just been kind of looking, well, anyway, I got to go, and, uh, I was just working today, trying to a, you know, uh, trying to get together just enough money for a quarter pounder, or somethin' and uh, you know, kind of want to get something in my stomach, there, uh... I'm kind of hungry, you know, so, uh, I can only drink so much coffee—"

"I don't have any money on me," Lambert fudged.

"Well, jus-just a little bit, you, enough, you know, for a burger or something. A guy's got to eat—"

"How much money do you need, Scott?"

"Uh, well...five dollars would help."

"Here's a dollar—It's all I've got—"

His filthy fingers snatched the dollar away like a frog snagging a fly with his tongue.

Just then Old Man Carl Wilderman' pickup truck roared up the alley, scattering gravel and creating a cloud of dust. With the engine still running, Carl hopped out of his cab, reached around the seat and grabbed his shotgun. Wheeling around, he cocked the gun, pointed it at Scott, and yelled, "You get your lazy, stinking, cross-dressing carcass out of here and don't you come round here begging no more, or the only thing you'll be begging for is mercy! Go on, get going or I'll finish you off! C'mon, white trash! I'm going to count to ten and if your ass ain't gone, I'm gonna shoot it for you'. I'm tired of your crap, you long haired freak! 10-9-8-..."

Scott's eyes opened wide, darting about in their sockets, as he fidgeted his hands and feet.

Lambert expected Carl to miss count 10-9-8-0 and then fire away. As soon as Carl started counting, Scott ran off like a frightened cat, taking off in the opposite direction, quickly disappearing down the end of the alley heading towards the Purple Finch Café.

Old Man Wilderman lowered his weapon and started laughing as he placed the shotgun back in the rear truck window.

Jimmy started giggling and so did Lambert and Chip. What made them laugh so hard was seeing a long haired guy running down the street wearing a plaid jacket, bright god-awful green polyester women's pants two sizes too small, one yellow sock and one black sock, and red and blue bowling shoes, two sizes too large. He kept on running and turned at the end of the block without ever looking back.

I have been through some terrible things in my life,
some of which actually happened.
– Mark Twain

EUGENE AND THE HAUNTED TRAIN BRIDGE

The summer break was coming to an end and school would be starting the next week. Since it was the last week of summer break, Lambert, Chip, and Jimmy were already making plans for one of their famous all-nighters. At least they were famous in their estimation. The last nights of summer vacation were a sacred ritual for all of them, especially the last week of vacation. They had a ritual of vowing to camp out every night. They couldn't wait to stay up all night, listen to the crickets, katydids, and cicadae, watch the stars come out, see the moonrise, race down to the railroad crossing in the middle of the night to revel in the power of a passing train, and stay awake long enough to hear the first birds of morning and to witness the sunrise. Such an itinerary was the norm, common, and ordinary, yet it seemed to excite the boys beyond measure.

Lambert and Chip were extra lucky, too, because not only did they have a tent and sleeping bags, but their family owned a camping trailer. The camper sat in the driveway behind their house. In their youthfulness they had convinced their mother that it would be good for them to stay out in the trailer all night long. Their dad was so busy working that it seemed he didn't care much where they slept just so long as they slept.

The boys would pile into the trailer and talk. Lambert and Chip would sleep in one bed and Eugene and Jimmy in the other. Of course, no sleeping took place until *after* sunrise. Jimmy was short and chubby. Eugene was a tall and muscular six foot two, long-haired monster. It seemed like he had been six-two since he was twelve years old. Several times throughout a night they would rouse from sleep when Eugene would slap Jimmy for getting too close under the covers or for passing gas and flapping the blankets. Poor Jimmy ended up on the floor on more than one occasion.

When Lambert and Chip's cousin Daniel would come to visit and spend the night with them in the trailer, Eugene would sleep on the floor. That way Daniel and Jimmy shared the bed. However, Eugene made it very clear that if anyone stepped on him he would kill that person dead – as if anybody was stupid enough to step on him. Unfortunately Daniel was an only child and he didn't deal very well with sharing a room, let alone a bed.

One night the summer before, Daniel had pulled all the covers off Jimmy and when Jimmy tried to pull them back to his side of the bed Daniel kicked him. Jimmy rolled off the end of the bed and fell on top of Eugene who was sleeping on the floor. Jimmy's right knee smashed Eugene in the groin. Suddenly everyone was wide awake, scrambling for cover. Eugene threw Jimmy out the trailer door on the gravel driveway.

* * * * *

Grandpa McChesney had purchased Lambert and Chip's mom a police scanner for her birthday so she could pass the time by keeping up with what was going on in Preston Point. So now the boys had to be careful because the slightest call for the police in their neighborhood would bring their mom out of the house to the camper.

Without exception, Mrs. McChesney would come out to the trailer and check on the boys before she'd go to bed for the night. They'd be chomping at the bit, ready to go and create monsters of chaos in their neighborhood by bugging the roomers, rapping trash cans with rocks, breaking empty beer bottles in the trash pits, or shooting off bottle rockets down the alley. They couldn't wait to burst out of the trailer and be in charge of town, or at least their corner of town. In their minds it was the world. Just to think that they'd be a few of the only ones awake in the whole city thrilled them.

Whenever their mom finally came outside they'd act like they were either groggy or asleep. Several times they'd all arrange to be under the covers, with the lights out, acting like they were sound asleep so that when she'd open the trailer door she'd know what good boys they were.

"Oh, boys, you shouldn't go to sleep with the camper door unlocked," she said upon coming out.

"Uh...oh...Yeah," Lambert answered in his best groggy voice, "Thanks Mom...G'night."

"G'night, Ma," Chip added.

"Is Daniel in there with you?" she asked, even though she saw him an hour before.

"Yeah, but he's sleeping," Lambert lied.

"Okay. Aunt Jean just called and wanted to make sure he wasn't out running the streets," she explained. "There are too many hoodlums out."

"The hoodlums," Daniel breathed out in a whisper from under the covers. "God, am I ever baby-fied!"

"Are the other boys in there?"

"Yeah, but we're real tired...we're sleeping...see you, mom. Make sure you turn the back porch light off." Lambert said.

"Okay, honey. Goodnight, Lambert. G'night Chip."

They listened as she walked through the gravel around to the backdoor.

"Danny, your mommy's calling you," Eugene snickered.

"Oh, Mama's boy—" Jimmy said with a laughing.

"Ha, like you got room to talk—'Daddy's boy'," Eugene interrupted him. "Why don't you just shut up? Your old man would beat you within an inch of your life if he e'er caught you out running around after curfew."

"No way!" Jimmy protested.

"Don't give me that guff. You know it's true!" Eugene gloated.

"Shut up, weasel breath," Jimmy threatened. "What about your dad?"

Eugene said nothing as he stared through Jimmy. Then in an unusually restrained monotone he said, "You don't know my dad. Leave him alone." He turned away as if lost in thought.

"C'mon guys, quiet down!" Lambert argued with a low whisper.

They waited and waited and waited, listening to their own breath until they heard the creak of the hinges on the backdoor and the click of the light switch. Then everything went black. They heard the door shut and their mom bolting the door behind her.

Before long Eugene and Jimmy were into another argument.

"Is, too," Eugene argued.

"Is not!" Jimmy insisted

"Is, too!" Eugene persisted.

"No it's not. Elmer Fudd isn't the guy who says 'ebede, ebebe, that's all folks.' That's Porky Pig!" argued Jimmy.

"No it's not! Porky's the dude with the shotgun."

"No, you got 'em mixed up, man. Elmer's the one who's bald and he's always out hunting for Bugs Bunny and—"

"No, that's that short red-headed guy with a mustache—"

"No! That's Yosemite Sam—" Chip interrupted Jimmy and Eugene.

"Jimmy's loony, man!" Eugene argued.

"No, I'm not. I just know what I'm talking about," Jimmy protested.

"Okay smarty-pants, How come Wiley Coyote never dies?" Eugene asked. "I mean he gets his face blown off and the next minute there he is, not a scratch on him."

"It's just a cartoon, Eugene!" Jimmy answered. "Besides, who cares? It's funny."

"I don't know, Jimmy. I mean if I fell off a cliff like he does, I'd be dead. What if some kid thought they could fly off the cliff like Wiley Coyote? Would that be funny?"

"Well, Eugene, most people know the difference between a cartoon and reality—unless you're confused."

"I ought to kick your puny butt—"

"C'mon guys it's just a show," Chip reminded them.

"Yeah, I know, but didn't you ever wonder about that kind of stuff when you were a kid?" Eugene asked.

"Not really—" Jimmy answered, but Chip and Lambert nodded their heads.

"One whole night I lay in bed wondering where Mr. Roger's neighborhood was," Chip said.

"Yeah, where was Mr. Rogers's neighborhood?" Lambert asked.

"And what was his real job, huh?" Chip asked. "And what was the deal with that stop and go traffic light in his house? I heard about a college kid who had one of those in his house and the cops arrested him!"

"Yeah, I think some of them shows can give a kid brain damage," Eugene asserted.

"Brain damage?! How's that?" Jimmy asked incredulously.

"The people on Sesame Street couldn't get off their block. They never went anywhere—"

"And what was Oscar's deal?" Jimmy asked.

"There was some kid somewhere," Eugene continued, "I heard about this on T.V. one night—anyway, this kid wouldn't clean his room because Oscar was his favorite character and his mom and dad had to take him to a shrink because he wouldn't take a bath or clean his room!"

"What about Big Bird? What was he—a guy or a girl?" Jimmy asked.

"I don't know. That always bugged me, too," Chip said.

"What was the deal with Bert and Ernie? Were they like

supposed to be *The Odd Couple* or were they orphans?" Jimmy asked.

"I just thought they were two guys without legs!" Chip snapped back.

"I heard Bert and Ernie were queers, man!" Eugene said.

"Don't say that—Bert and Ernie were my favorite characters," Lambert said.

"See, I told you guys," Eugene laughed. "Chip, you better watch yourself when you're sleeping in the same bed with him."

"Oh, shut up, Eugene," Lambert said. "I am *not* queer."

"And what was the deal with that Frog and that Pig—" Eugene asked.

"Kermit and Miss Piggy?" Chip asked.

"Some sick stuff, man," said Eugene

"My old man told me they were teaching kids to have mixed marriages between blacks and whites—" said Jimmy.

"Oh, gee—" Lambert sighed, "Sesame Street was a good show. And I liked Mr. Rogers, too."

"Yeah, you would. He's queer, too." Eugene snapped.

"No, he's not!" Lambert said. "I always hoped that Mr. Rogers would walk over to Sesame Street one day—"

"What for? To play with Bert and Ernie?" Eugene quipped.

"Forget it," Lambert said as he threw up his hands.

Momentarily they stopped talking to hear what sounded like an air raid siren. It turned out to be a car horn that must have been stuck. It reminded Lambert of the threat of nuclear war.

"You guys ever take time to think about how close we are to total annihilation?" Lambert asked.

"Not really," Eugene seemed to boast.

"I do, but if I think about for too long I can't sleep at night," offered Jimmy.

"Grandpa says that if we knew what was being hauled through town in boxcars and tanker cars, you wouldn't sleep at night," Lambert said.

"Is that why sometimes I wake up in the middle of the night and think I'm dead?" Jimmy asked.

"No, Jimmy. It's because you don't have a brain," said Eugene as he poked him in the ribs.

"No, really guys," Lambert continued. "I'm serious. I'm talking about the all the nuclear arms. There are missiles everywhere."

"Yeah. I'll bet there's an underground missile launcher in Mabel's back yard," Jimmy laughed.

"Well, Reagan's asleep half the time and he carries the black briefcase with him all the time—" Lambert began.

"What black briefcase?" Eugene asked.

"You know, *the briefcase, the nuclear football*," Lambert answered knowingly, "with all the remote control buttons for the nuclear missiles."

"No doubt?" Eugene asked.

"See? Kind of freaks you out, doesn't it?" Lambert replied.

"Yeah." Eugene said.

"Brezhnev's got one, too," Lambert continued.

"Who's he?" Eugene asked.

"The leader of the Soviet Union."

"We need more nukes!" Chip said loudly.

Jimmy looked as if he was in a daze.

"Now Jimmy don't go thinking of killing yourself," Eugene said. "There ain't no bombs going to kill you tonight—"

"You don't know that, Eugene," Lambert interrupted. "It could happen tonight and—"

"Shut up! You guys are freaking me out," Jimmy said.

"We're just telling you what your tax dollars are going for," Lambert continued. "I heard when President Reagan got shot nobody knew what to do with the briefcase! I even heard there were a couple minutes after he got shot that the Soviets were thinking of launching an attack. I'll even bet there's a red phone and a white phone in the president's limousine and in his office."

What're they for?" Jimmy asked.

"Well the white one's connected to the Vatican so when "Ronbo Ray-Gun" pushes the buttons one day he can call the pope." And in his best attempt at an impersonation of Reagan, Lambert began, "'Yes, is this Pope John Paul? Yeah, well this is President Reagan in Washington. Yes, I'm glad you asked that question. In about fifteen minutes the world's going to start exploding. Uh huh, I pushed the buttons and started World War III. Well, yes, I know the Russian people will die, but they are Atheistic Communists—"

The guys giggled as Eugene asked, "Where's the red phone go?"

"The Kremlin. That way Reagan can call up ol' man Brezhnev and say, 'Uh, yes, is your father home? You are, oh, I see...you sound so young...Well, this is President Reagan. I know I called you for something...Oh, yeah, now I remember. I was eating some of my jelly beans, you know they're my favorite. Anyway, Nancy and I were just looking out over Washington when I thought I saw an incoming missile. Nancy tried to convince me it wasn't, but I must've been dreaming or something, and I thought you all had sent the missiles over, so I pushed all the buttons in my briefcase. Anyhow, Nancy and I wanted to be the first to tell you that we really didn't mean anything by it, so when all the smoke clears over there, we'll have to do lunch. And I'll send you some of my best jelly beans.' Couldn't you hear it?"

"So, uh, like you're saying I'll be lucky if I live to see my graduation from high school?" Eugene pondered.

"I wouldn't say that," Lambert said.

"Stupid Communists," Eugene replied.

"Well, what about us?" Lambert asked. "We keep on making more and more nuclear missiles. I mean how many times can you blow up the earth?"

"Our science teacher at school told us that we've stockpiled enough of an arsenal to blow the world up nine times!" Chip said.

"Cool!" Eugene said.

"What about that guy who tried to kill Reagan?" Jimmy asked.

"Yeah, where were you when you heard the president got shot?" Lambert asked.

"I just got home from school and was watching T.V. Where were you Lambert?" Jimmy asked.

"We were getting ready for baseball practice and we all heard it on the radio. I just sat there for a few minutes in shock. People talk about the day Kennedy got shot and people can still remember the day and know exactly where they were and what they were doing when they heard about it on the news. It reminded me of that," Lambert said.

Eugene spoke up, "I didn't find out 'til the next day at school."

"Then they tried to kill the pope," Chip said.

"Probably a Communist plot—" offered Eugene.

"Probably?! I'll bet it was the KGB!" Lambert declared.

"My dad says the pope is a communist," Jimmy said.

"He is *not* a communist!" Lambert railed.

"Who cares, we're all going to burn anyway!" Eugene remarked with a laugh.

"Yeah, you know things are getting out of hand when they're out trying to kill the pope." Chip said.

"Okay guys, are we just going to sit here and mope around about the end of the world and talk all night or are we going to go out and stir up some trouble?" Eugene challenged them.

"Yeah, I'm ready to go commit suicide before Reagan does it for me," Lambert said sarcastically.

"I don't want to be around when the nukes start flying in!" Jimmy whined.

"Just quit worrying about the nukes, dude. Let's have some fun," Eugene cheerfully said.

"What about the cops?" Daniel asked.

"What about Goofy?" Jimmy asked.

"Don't be worrying about that dumb dog—I want to tangle with Spikey boy!!" Eugene exclaimed, as if last week's run in with Spike was only hors d'oeurves. "I'll turn his dog into goofy-burgers."

"Who's Spike?" Daniel asked.

"Just some dumb cop who thinks he's General Patton," Eugene laughed.

"Remember the time those University guys drove off in his police car and took his dumb dog, Goofy?" Jimmy asked.

"Yeah, they finally found Goofy in the john at McDonald's with his two front legs handcuffed together," Lambert answered. "And the Sherriff's department found his car in the Red River the next day. There was a picture of it on the front page of the paper. And he promised that he was going to find the kids who did it!"

"What about the time when he pulled over a speeder and left his driver's side door open?" Chip said.

"And a friend of the guy he had pulled over drove by and ripped Spike's door off!" Jimmy finished the story. They all laughed.

"Yeah, he always wears those silver shades, too," Eugene laughed. "Thinks he's Hollywood. Hill Street Blues."

"Chips," said Jimmy.

"Chumps," Eugene corrected Jimmy.

"Adam-Twelve," Chip said.

"Barney-Fife," said Jimmy.

"Yeah, but they don't even give him a bullet," Lambert said.

They grew quiet and Eugene broke the silence. "I've got an idea."

One could always tell when one of Eugene's great ideas was

coming on by the gravelly sound in his voice and his unblinking eyes. "Let's go down to the river and walk across the train bridge!" He looked at each of the guys.

They each stared back. None of them said a word.

"C'mon, guys." Eugene said as he got up off the bed and reached over to turn on a light.

"No way!" Lambert said. "Not the railroad bridge."

"You crazy, 'Gene?" asked Jimmy, "We might fall in the river and drown!"

"That's suicide, Eugene," Chip exclaimed. "What if our Mom finds out?!"

"You bunch a wussies!" Eugene fired back, "What're you going to do, stay in here and play with yourselves all night?"

"No!" Jimmy shot back. "We're going to go out for a walk and – you know – kick some cans, knock over a few trash cans and stir up some trouble."

"Oh, like that's really some trouble. You're just too cool, Jimmy-boy," Eugene said as he threw his pillow at Jimmy. "Now, get your shoes on and let's go – all of you," he ordered.

Daniel had been sitting there wide-eyed, but at that he finally spoke up, "We can't do that. You guys can't do any of that. The cops will be after us."

"That's why you do it, dumb-head," Eugene said as he straightened his back and nodded. "It's great watching these stupid cops chase us. They think were burglars or car thieves."

"That's what I mean, they're liable to shoot us," Daniel said.

"Eh, don't worry 'bout it—they can't shoot straight! Plus they need the excitement," Eugene boldly said. "That's the only reason they became cops."

"Either that or they just like to eat doughnuts," Chip added.

"Or so they could play with the red lights and siren," Jimmy said.

"Yeah, you ever notice how many firemen are pyromaniacs?"

Lambert asked. "They love fires and stuff and when there aren't enough fires they go set things on fire and burn things up just so they can have a fire run!"

"What about the railroad police? They patrol that bridge." Daniel persisted, returning to the subject of the train bridge.

"Now, be serious," Eugene asked. "Have you ever seen any cops patrolling the railroad tracks?"

None of them answered him.

"No, right? See? Just ignore him, guys," Eugene said as he waved his hand, brushing Daniel aside. "Okay, guys, it's time for the train bridge. What do you say?"

The four of them stared at Eugene at first, but then Daniel spoke up, "I'm not going."

"Say *what?*" Eugene sniped.

"I'm going to sleep. I ain't going to walk over no bridge in the middle of the night!"

"Oh, *yes* you *are,*" Eugene exclaimed.

"No I'm not. I'll just go home. I'm not going to cross a train bridge."

"You're not going home. You're going to stay with us, boy," Eugene threatened, "And when we get to that bridge you're going to be right there with me–"

"Who says?" Daniel interrupted.

"I do!" Eugene lunged at Daniel and tried to strangle him.

"Okay! Okay!" Daniel yelled as he fought off Eugene's grip. "But if I get caught, you're going to pay for it!"

"Oh, like I'm really scared!" He held his hands out for all to see. "Look guys, I'm shaking! At least I'm not the one who pooped his panties!!! Eugene laughed.

"What?" he asked.

"Didn't you just poop your pants, Danny?" Eugene asked.

"No!" he protested.

"Then why are you shaking, baby?"

"Uh, we don't have to, uh, we don't really have to walk

across the bridge, do we Eugene?" Chip half-heartedly asked. "I mean, can't we just like, go there, and say we did?"

"Son—of–a–!" Eugene blew up. "What a bunch of Wussies!"

"No, I think you ought to listen to him, Eugene," Lambert tried to reason with him. "You know that bridge is haunted."

"No way! I can't believe you, Lambert! There ain't no ghost there."

"Several railroaders, engineers, and passengers have reported seeing the ghost of a lady in a wedding dress on the bridge at night –"

"The widowed bride," Eugene said with a laugh. "I've heard the stories. Her fiancé was killed in the war so she put on her wedding dress and committed suicide by throwing herself in front of a train. They're all lies, stories to keep kids like you guys off the bridge at night."

"Okay, even if there's no ghost, there are bums living under that bridge," Chip continued.

"Yeah—drug addicts, too!" Jimmy added enthusiastically.

"You've got to listen to them, Eugene—they might cut our ears off–" Daniel argued.

"Shut up, wimp!" Eugene said, shaking his head, "Man, that's it. I'm goin' home!" He grabbed his pillow and blanket.

"No, don't man. Don't go, Eugene!—we'll do it!" Lambert boldly proclaimed as Eugene headed for the door, "Don't leave. We'll do it."

"Speak for yourself," Daniel said with a kick to Lambert's knee.

"Real smart," Chip whispered under his breath, "Bertrum. Real smart!"

"Okay, let's go!" Eugene clapped his hands.

"Yeah, let's get going guys," Lambert said, spurring them on. Chip and Jimmy tied their shoes as Daniel stiffly moved towards the door, cowering away from the hulk of Eugene. By now it was 12:45 in the morning when they opened the door of the trailer, put on their baseball caps, and ventured out into the darkened alley.

"Cool," Jimmy breathed out, "we're going to break curfew."

"We already are, you idiot," said Eugene as he led the way toward the intersection of Bonaventure and Powell.

"What if my dad sees me?" Jimmy worried out loud.

"Your old man's in bed," assured Eugene.

"How do you know that? You don't know that. He might be up just waitin' for me to mess up! I told him I was going to stay all night at the McChesney's, but he—"

"Shhh!!!" Eugene swung his arm around and hushed Jimmy's mouth, "Car—"

It was a police car on Bonaventure Boulevard. Car seventy-seven. Sergeant Spike and his dog, Goofy.

"Oh" Daniel moaned loudly while the rest scrambled for cover.

Eugene reeled around and looked at Daniel. Daniel froze and didn't make another peep.

Spike was smoking a cigarette; his driver's window was rolled down.

"He's just out patrolling. Nothing to lose your bowels over, nit-wits," Eugene sniped, addressing all. "Let's just cross the street and act like you know what you're doing!"

"B-b-but, but that was S-S-Spike," Jimmy whined and stuttered, "What if he saw us—"

"So?" Eugene rolled his eyes. "Don't worry 'bout it...."

They heard male voices and a rattling noise like the clank of a chain. A couple of college guys in t-shirts and jeans were at the Sinclair station getting drinks from the Double Cola vending machine. They were smoking and talking loudly as they crossed the street and walked a few feet from the boys; their cigarette smoke lingered in the air. Lambert and the others stayed in the shadow of the tree-lined side street until the college guys moved on before attempting to cross Bonaventure Avenue.

A line of vehicles waiting at the stoplight at Hickman Street headed their direction when the signal turned green; a delivery truck and a bus noisily passed by. When the street cleared Eugene herded them across as he led them to the haunted train bridge.

* * * * *

Lambert heard dogs barking that he'd never heard before and noises that came from he didn't know where: cats fighting or mating behind trash cans, hooting owls, and whistling birds in the moonlight. Every time they'd hear or see a car or truck, they'd duck behind a parked car or a hedgerow. Lambert imagined that each homeowner was watching their every move and he could feel their eyes focused on them as Eugene recklessly took them down the primrose path of an alley.

Lambert followed after Eugene, Chip, and Jimmy while behind trailed Daniel. He was walking slowly and checking behind his back every few seconds, all the while making unnecessary noise with his feet in the gravel.

"Stop dragging your feet, Daniel Boone?!" Eugene turned about and whispered loudly to Daniel. "Lift your feet when you walk, dodo."

"Lambert, I'm telling your mom when we get back–" Daniel informed everyone.

"I thought you were the one who wanted to camp out," Lambert asked.

Daniel didn't say anything.

When they got to the end of the block they stopped and looked to Eugene. Eugene led them across the side street and neared Jimmy's house. Jimmy came unglued, "No! Don't go this way. My dad will see me! Don't go down my alley!"

Just then they heard someone walking. They froze. Eugene pointed to the edge of some bushes and he jumped over. Lambert and the others all followed suit and jumped over them, landing on the other side of Jimmy's yard. Daniel unfortunately scratched himself since he was only wearing shorts.

"Why'd you have to make us jump, Eugene?" Daniel whined, breaking the silence, "I cut myself!"

"Who the heck told you to wear shorts?" Eugene whispered.

"I didn't know," Daniel quietly answered. "It's summer. I didn't know we were going to escape from Alcatraz."

"What a jackass! Lambert, is he really your cousin?" Eugene asked as he shook his head.

Jimmy waved and swung his arms in a poor attempt to get the two to stop talking. "Shut up, guys! My dad's asleep!" Jimmy said as he pointed towards his house, "My dad's bedroom window is right there!"

All at once, walking ten feet from them was the roomer Larry Brown. Where he came from Lambert didn't know, but Larry walked by slowly, his shoulders slouching as usual as he hummed a little tune. He had no idea that he was being watched. The boys all looked at each other.

Lambert could barely keep from bursting out laughing as he whispered ever so softly, "Grubby". Jimmy heard him and snorted out a noise.

Larry stopped. His feet swished in the gravel, and his eyes darted to and fro in search of the source of the noise. He stood motionless for about ten seconds and then he started walking away. The boys were saved. Or so Lambert thought.

That's when Lambert, out of the corner of his eye, saw Eugene reaching for a brick. Going up on his knees, Eugene reared back to heave the brick. Lambert said, "No!" but it was too late. Eugene threw the brick at Old Man Wilderman's trash cans. It crashed into one can knocking it into the other, making a loud clanging commotion.

Larry reeled around to look only to turn back and run away.

Old Man Wilderman's bedroom light came on and they could see his shadow scrambling about, raising the blinds, and pulling the curtains to the side. He was shouting loudly.

Jimmy gasped noisily when he saw the naked body of his father plastered against the window. Jimmy panted as if the wind had been knocked out of him. Jimmy kept saying, "I'm dead. He's going to kill me! I'm dead. He's going to kill me!"

Eugene laughed.

"You dumb-head! We'll all be dead. Run!" Jimmy warned, as he ran frantically across the street in the opposite direction of Larry Brown. "If we don't run now, you'll be picking buckshot out of your butt till Christmas!"

The others ran across the street and through the alley where they hid in an old garage. Lambert could see both ways for two blocks and everything was quiet. Larry had probably gone back to the Weaver's Boarding House.

"Let's go back and get him!" Eugene giggled.

"Are you crazy, Eugene?" Jimmy asked. "You just woke my old man up. He'll see me! He's probably already outside with his shotgun!"

"You're pathetic," Eugene shook his head.

"What if Merle comes out with his shotgun?" Lambert asked.

"Who cares?" Eugene replied. "He just sits on his porch and gets drunk."

Eugene had a point; Merle usually did fall asleep in his chair drinking whiskey.

"Let's go get Larry." Eugene persisted.

"Are you nuts, man?" asked Chip, "That's right next door to our house."

"It don't matter," Eugene snapped.

They all followed Eugene down the alley with Daniel trailing behind.

"Now where are we going?" Daniel asked Eugene as he caught up with him.

"We're going to go spook the grubworm," Eugene proudly proclaimed. "I owe him one anyway since he called the cops on me."

"But you threw an axe at him!" Jimmy said.

"Your point?" Eugene smiled.

"Aw, man. I'm going back to the trailer and get some sleep," Daniel told Eugene. "I ain't going to get shot at or have the cops chasing me.".

"Good!" Eugene quickly replied, trying to slap Daniel. "We didn't want any girls with us anyway."

"Aren't you funny. Ha, ha." Daniel rolled his eyes as he darted away from Eugene's hand.

"Maybe we'll start having some fun now. Bye, bye, cry baby!" Eugene taunted.

Daniel stomped down the alley and walked behind the McChesney's garage towards the trailer.

"Okay guys, grab a few rocks and boulders—a brick if you can find one," Eugene said.

They all sneaked through the neighbors' yards and crawled into Eugene's backyard. Eugene then launched an assault of stones on the speed limit sign between his house and the Weavers' Boarding House. One of the rocks crashed loudly into the sign and instantly Larry Brown shot up off the porch swing and leaned over the banister.

"Grubby's back on the porch, guys!" Eugene chuckled. "Watch this." He took a brick and threw it at the street sign again. It crashed loudly, right on target.

Larry walked down the stairs and stood on the front step looking their direction.

Eugene yelled as loud as he could, "GRUBWORM!"

"What was that for?!" Jimmy exploded in a wheeze. "Aw, my Gawd! Here he comes!"

"Cool!" Eugene said with a smile as he ran off toward the alley.

Lambert, Chip, and Jimmy followed. Jimmy struggled to keep up with Chip and Lambert; Eugene was way ahead. He had shoes on tonight which made him an even faster runner. He was the only kid Lambert and Chip ever knew who could outrun anyone barefooted.

"Let's go behind the Weavers' house and wait–" Eugene panted out.

"No way!" Jimmy interrupted. "He'll see us! He's probably already called the cops!"

"No, he'll never suspect we came back here," Eugene explained.

"We'll wait for ol' Grubby to go up to his room—and then we'll throw a brick through his window!" Eugene gleefully plotted.

"Aw, I don't know, Eugene," Chip said.

"Merle's liable to be out there with his shotgun," Lambert added.

"What about the railroad bridge?" Chip asked.

"Yeah, what about the train bridge?" Jimmy stammered, as if trying to sound tough.

Those were Lambert's sentiments as well; the train bridge seemed like a mild escapade compared to harassing Larry Brown.

"Hey—we got all night, man," Eugene said, extending his arms out and holding his thumbs up, "and I'm just getting started."

"What if Larry finds out it's us? He'll call the cops on you again," Chip said.

"On *me*? What about *you*?" Eugene shot back.

"Yeah, but what if he *already* called the cops?" Jimmy asked.

"Bring 'em on," Eugene braved. "We'll just run and hide! Now stop worrying – all of you."

They then crept behind the Weavers' house to get in position.

"Oh, God, we're going to die—look!" said Chip, pointing towards the street. Illuminated in the headlights of a slow moving car was the roomer, Larry, standing on the sidewalk in front of the boarding house.

"There he is!" Lambert said.

Eugene handed Lambert half a brick and said, "Aim at that piece of tin covering the old coal chute." Together they heaved their brick chunks and both of them pounded on top of the metal sheet making a loud cracking noise which shattered the silence. Jimmy and Chip ran to the side of the garage as Eugene and Lambert hid in the trash pit. But in the process of scrambling to hide they lost sight of Larry.

Lambert peeked around to see if Larry might be coming up behind, but he didn't see a thing. Suddenly Lambert noticed that a light came on in the upstairs hallway of the boarding house. Another light appeared in one of the upper rooms. Larry was in his room; he took his shirt off, turned off his light, looked out his window and lit up a cigarette.

Without warning, Eugene bellowed out in a deep, hoarse scream, "Larry! Grubworm!

Larry leaned out his open window and yelled out, "I know who you are and where you live! And I've already called the cops!! The landlord's waiting for you too!"

"See, I told you, numbskull!" Jimmy yelled at Eugene.

"Run!!" Eugene yelled. By now Chip and Jimmy were heading towards the trailer, but Eugene ran towards the end of the alley and Lambert followed him. Chip and Jimmy turned back and headed the same direction. When they all arrived at the end of the block, Eugene said, "Okay, guys, *now* it's time to go to the railroad bridge."

"What about Daniel?" Lambert asked.

"Forget him. He went to bed," answered Eugene, "Maybe the Grubworm will get him! I'll deal with him later in my own way. We're going to the train bridge tonight—"

Jimmy looked queasy and said, "Tonight? Do we have to? Can't we just go back to Lambert and Chip's and get some sleep?"

"Sleep? No, you wimp. We're all in on this," Eugene barked, "Otherwise, you can go back and crawl in the sack with Daniel. Now, are you in or not?"

None of them dared challenge Eugene's authority. Lambert looked at his watch and it was nearly two-thirty in the morning.

They made their way through people's yards, evading barking dogs and houses with burning porch lights. They crossed every street without incident until they got to Riverside drive. A slow moving car started their direction.

"Cop!" Jimmy yelled out and they all dove for cover. As the car passed by it turned out only to be a taxicab; the unlit advertisement boards on the cab's roof looked like a bar of emergency lights. They stood, dusted themselves off, and proceeded to run across Riverside. No sooner had they crossed over when they were at the tracks. And there it was—the train bridge. Lambert looked at his watch in the street light; it was nearly three a.m.

Lambert couldn't believe they were at the railroad bridge. And yet all the time that they were heading towards the railroad bridge Lambert was praying that a train would come so they wouldn't have to cross the bridge and risk life and limb. He knew they were all scared—except for Eugene; Eugene wasn't scared of anything.

Besides the fear of a ghost, Lambert feared that there might be a bum or a wino or a drug dealer under the bridge. But he didn't see anyone, or hear anyone under the bridge once he got to the levee.

Eugene cheered as he ordered them all out onto the bridge, "Whew, wee!! All right—let's walk across, boys!" Incredibly, he started running out on the bridge. He was wearing sneakers, so he was making good time. Jimmy was inching his way along the ties, when he began yelling for help, "Chip! Chip! Lambert! Help me! My shoe's stuck!! My foot got twisted under the rail!!

In between Jimmy's screams, Lambert thought he heard a train whistle. Lambert had boldly gone out about fifteen feet from the base of the bridge, kind of dilly-dallying to make it look like he was really walking across the bridge in case Eugene were to question his manhood.

Just as Chip made it over to Jimmy, Lambert heard the distinct sound of an inbound freight train: the tolling of an engine's bell and the whine of engines on their ascent to the bridge. Lambert yelled: "Train!"

Eugene was already at least half-way out in the middle of the bridge, "Guys, get out here! I see the ghost! She's in her wedding gown!" That's when Lambert heard the train whistle again, and he could see the headlight beam searching the cornfields and sky on the other side of the bridge.

Lambert heard the engineer blow the horn at one of the last grade crossings before crossing the bridge. The clangor of steel on steel jolted him as the rails began to ping and pop and sing as the bridge itself moaned under the impending weight. Hopping over Jimmy and Chip, Lambert ran back to safety.

Meanwhile, Chip was still wrestling to get Jimmy's foot free from between two pieces of rail and a railroad tie. Jimmy was crying as the train engines began to bear down on the bridge. The trestles started shaking and the whining engines and clanging bells murdered the silent night.

By now Eugene was aware of his predicament and he was desperately trying to get back across. The headlights kept getting brighter and brighter as Eugene ran hard with the train right behind him. The air horns began to blast, non-stop: one long continual blast. Lambert screamed for Eugene to get clear of the bridge.

Suddenly Jimmy's foot was free and both he and Chip leapt away from the roadbed of rails and ties, but they could barely endure the blinding light, the rumbling engines, and deafening horns. Just when Eugene should have jumped off the tracks, he disappeared from sight.

It all happened so fast, it was hard to make out. Lambert couldn't see whether Eugene had been hit and thrown off the trestle, or whether he fell under the train and was cut to shreds. It was at that moment they all had to roll down the hill, and scramble into the weeds alongside the roadbed of ballast, as the locomotives roared by, horns blaring into the death of night. Lambert prayed for Eugene as the clangoring train thundered by.

The three engine freight train didn't slow down at all. All Lambert could think of was Eugene – and the fact that he was dead.

* * * * *

Eugene Thomas was dead. Of that Lambert was certain. He had been scraped off the bridge and spread like peanut butter on the rails. There was no question, he was splattered everywhere. His head was likely stuck on the freight engine's front coupler and his brains were in the river. It was a quick death. At least he didn't have to suffer.

Or worse—he was in the river, bleeding, hemorrhaging, drowning, washing away in agonizing torture.

We got him killed, Lambert thought. *It's our fault. It would have never happened if we hadn't decided to leave the trailer. What's left of Eugene is strewn up and down that bridge, between here and the street crossing. Any guts left over are on the rails. Once the train passes, we're going to find his body—hunks and chunks of it—up and down the tracks. I'll never be able to hear another train without thinking of Eugene. I'll never be able to cross another bridge without thinking of Eugene.*

I'm an accomplice to reckless homicide. Manslaughter, Lambert thought to himself. *O God, help me*, Lambert may have prayed aloud, but he couldn't recall. Even if he did, the train was too loud for the guys to hear him. *Eugene's family is going to sue my mom and dad. Now I **am** dead.*

I just hope he went to Heaven.

These and other thoughts filled Lambert's mind in those following split seconds.

The train was so long, a veritable train from hell. It seemed it had two-hundred cars if not five hundred. *When's it going to end?* he asked, alone with the dilemma. *A train from hell* killed Eugene.

Finally the sound began to lessen and the caboose rolled by; Lambert watched the lone conductor standing on the caboose's porch as if looking for some pesky kids who were trying to climb the bridge. The blinking red light on the end of the caboose glowed on and off as the end of the train disappeared around the curve going off into town.

Lambert then turned and stared up at the bridge—that cold, silent, empty, rusty, black, graffiti-drenched, haunted bridge. He didn't want to venture up the roadbed, but he knew he had to do something.

He had to find Eugene – dead or alive. No, all three of them had to find Eugene.

Lambert's heart throbbed in his chest and his temples ached; Chip's face was emotionless, white with shock; and Jimmy's chin was quivering. They never said a word as they looked high and low, side to side, over the bridge and the tracks, in the water, in the weeds, and along the rocky roadbed.

They knew exactly what and who they were looking for, but how does one absorb the violent death of a friend who was alive and joking with you just moments before?

"Answer us, Eugene!" Lambert called out.

Hoping against hope they all three cried out simultaneously, "Eugene! Eugene!"

There was no answer. Eugene was not there.

"Eugene! Where are you, man?!!" Jimmy looked and sounded as if he was about to cry.

"Can you hear us, Eugene?!" Lambert called out louder. Still no answer. All he could hear was the echoing groan and lonely moan of the disappearing freight train.

Lambert motioned for Jimmy and Chip to walk towards the bridge. So they slowly walked out on the bridge where they had last seen Eugene alive, about thirty feet out. There was no sign of him. Lambert looked in the cracks between the ties and up and down the sides of the bridge, but there was no Eugene. It was dark under the bridge so he couldn't see anything there. He looked in the river for signs of his body but in the cloudy moonlight he only saw water. Lambert didn't particularly want to find Eugene, or find what was left of him. But they had to look for him. He was their friend. At least he used to be.

Lambert kept thinking of Eugene in the past tense and he felt terrible for doing so. He looked and looked and still there was no trace of him.

There was an eerily loud silence, a terrible absence of city noise — even the crickets and frogs were mute. Suddenly Lambert was distracted by fluttering movement overhead and several bats swooped down near him, their wings beating the night air. He covered his head with his hands and dodged the bats.

"Oh Gawd!" Jimmy squawked, covering his head with his hands and dropping to his knees while Chip ducked down.

The bats flapped away as quickly as they had come.

"It's an omen!" Jimmy said with great fear as he stood again.

Chip, visibly shaken, said with a slight stutter, "Lambert, let's go home."

"We can't leave a man behind, Chip," Lambert asserted himself. "Eugene wouldn't leave us behind, would he?"

"Yeah," both Chip and Jimmy answered at the same time.

"Never mind," Lambert said with a nervous laugh as they started to walk the tracks back into town. Jimmy trailed behind, walking backwards half the way, looking behind himself, calling out for Eugene every so often. Still there were no signs of body parts or clothing or shoes on the tracks. Once they left the tracks they were wordless.

Halfway back to the trailer, they started running. Lambert was unsure who started running first, Chip or Jimmy, but whoever did got them all running.

The reality of Eugene's disappearance had set its hook.

"He's dead!" Jimmy cried out. "The bats are a sign from God he's dead! He's dead! Eugene got killed! Eugene died tonight! Oh, God, man! Eugene died tonight! We got him killed!"

"Get a hold of yourself," Lambert begged Jimmy.

"My dad will kill me! Even though he didn't like Eugene,

he's still going to kill me for killing him!" Jimmy said as he fell to the ground mid-stride.

Lambert stopped in the middle of the street when he saw the headlights of several approaching vehicles; he grabbed Chip and Jimmy, pulling them in between two parked cars.

"Oh, God, Lambert, what're we going to do!" Chip whispered, "What if he *is* dead?"

"Shhh. Let me think....Maybe he was stuck on the side of the train or something. He might be down under the bridge just knocked unconscious or something. We'll find him. We'll find him. Come on, guys! I got a feeling he's still alive."

"Yeah, maybe he's still warm, in a death grip, stuck up under a train engine," Jimmy said angrily.

"Rigor-mortis' already set in, Lambert," lamented Chip.

"No, I'm serious," Lambert said, "We're going to find him. We've got to find him."

"No, *I'm serious*, Lamb—he's dead. Hang it up," Jimmy countered his optimism. "We got him killed. Face it. We should have never gone. We should have stayed in the trailer with Daniel."

"Daniel!" Lambert exclaimed, forgetting about him until Jimmy reminded me. "Daniel can help us!" Lambert tried to reassure Jimmy and Chip, "We're going to have to go get our bikes and ride up and down the tracks and see if we can find him. Eugene might've hung on to the train for a while before he fell off or some—"

"Lambert, shouldn't we call the cops?" Chip interrupted.

"No!" Lambert replied, "Then we'd all get in trouble for being out on the bridge!"

"Yeah, but we've got to call the cops since Eugene's a missing person," Jimmy argued.

"No," Chip answered, "—then we'd get Eugene in trouble—"

"Yeah, but he's already in trouble," Jimmy rejoined.

"Especially if he's *dead*."

"We don't know that. What if he isn't dead?" Lambert asked, "Are you willing to be the one to tell him you're the one who ratted on him for being on the bridge?"

"Heck, I don't know! I just ain't ever got nobody killed before," Jimmy shot back.

"Don't worry about it," Lambert argued, "That's what Eugene would say. When the sun starts to come up, we'll go back down by the river and look under the bridge and see if Eugene's down there. Look, guys, as long as we don't find a body, then he's still alive, right?"

There was a collective silence among them as the cars passed. None were police cars. Lambert stepped out into the street. All he could hear was the hum of a transformer on a streetlamp pole, some barking dogs in the distance, a car's squealing tires and a motorcyclist revving his engine on the boulevard.

They all started running again.

"Who's going to tell Daniel what happened to Eugene," Chip asked, winded.

"Not me," Jimmy quickly replied. "Lambert can do it."

Lambert didn't say anything but he began rehearsing his lines in his head, thinking of something to tell Daniel. He didn't think any of them were too worried about the cops seeing them. In fact, he doubted that any of them were thinking of Sergeant Spike as they ran down the middle of the street. All they were thinking about was how they lost Eugene. Lambert's hands were half numb and he felt like he was going to throw up.

When they got back to the camper it was four o'clock in the morning.

Lambert reached up and turned the knob on the trailer door, thinking of ways that he could awaken Daniel and break the news to him that Eugene was dead, killed by a freight train on the railroad bridge. As Lambert opened the door and stepped up into the trailer, Daniel was sitting up in bed, wide awake; his eyes were wide open and face ashen.

Before Lambert could tell him what had happened on the bridge and spill the horrible news, Daniel spoke.

"Lambert, Chip, your mom's looking for you."

"What do you mean?!" Lambert demanded. That's all he needed – more trouble for what was turning out to be the most terrible night of his life. Lambert repeated, "What do you mean, Daniel?"

"Man, your gooses are cooked! Your mom came out about an hour ago looking for you guys!"

"No she didn't!" Chip said, "You're lying!"

"She said the police got a call about some kids out messing around on the railroad bridge." He paused and turned to Jimmy. "Jimmy, your old man was down here, too."

"Oh, God. I'm dead. We're dead!" Jimmy said, holding his head.

"Lambert and Chip's mom called Jimmy's house to see if you all were down there," Daniel continued, "but since you weren't, your dad came down here looking for you. He's ticked. And he wants to know who threw those rocks at his trash cans."

"Are you messing with me?!" Jimmy asked as he held his stomach as if a wave of nausea hit him.

"Would I make this up? I don't think so. Your old man came down to find out where you were," Daniel answered. "He said the cops came down to his house looking for you too because one of the roomers called the cops. They thought you might've been involved in some vandalism."

"I'm a goner," Jimmy wheezed out.

"And the worst part of it all?" Daniel rhetorically asked. "You'll never believe which cop was here."

"Who?" All three of them asked simultaneously.

"Officer Spike—" Daniel laughed.

Chip moaned aloud.

"Oh, boy," Lambert exhaled slowly as he wringed his hands and cracked his knuckles.

"Son of a sausage biscuit! My ass is grass," cried Jimmy, "Where's my Dad now?"

"With Spike and Lambert and Chip's dad," Daniel explained, "They're probably down at the train bridge by now looking for you."

"You're a liar!" Jimmy threatened.

"Spike said he was going to find you and that Eugene Thomas kid," Daniel gloated.

"Oh, well. It really isn't that big of a deal, considering what we've been through tonight," Lambert pondered aloud.

"Don't be pulling any tricks on us, Daniel – especially after the kind of night we've had," Chip warned.

"What's that mean?" Daniel asked.

Chip and Jimmy looked at Lambert as if wanting him to be the harbinger of Eugene's demise.

"What's wrong guys?" Daniel persisted. "Where's Eugene?"

Lambert stared back at Jimmy and Chip.

"You guys look like you saw the ghost," Daniel's eyes were lidless. "Well? Did you?"

"You have no idea what we've just been through–" Lambert began, looking at Daniel.

"What're you talking about, Lambert?" asked Daniel, grabbing his flashlight. "Is Eugene all right?"

Lambert imagined that the three of them must have looked like angels of death.

"We were all down at the train bridge," Lambert began, "when Eugene got out in the middle—"

"Eugene's dead!" Jimmy yelled out, interrupting Lambert's narrative, "He died! He got killed!"

"He got ran over and his body's in the river," Chip added to thechaos.

"Oh, my God!" Daniel exclaimed. "What happened?"

"Come on guys! We're not sure he's dead," Lambert said, attempting to quell their fears. "We haven't found his body yet. He might've been sucked up under the train and he's hanging on or something."

"I'm sure of that," Jimmy said, his eyes opening even wider. "I hope I'm not the one to find his body."

"You guys are joking, right?" Daniel begged. "Aren't you?" Daniel paused and looked at each of them. "You're not joking, are you?"

"No," Lambert answered as he sat down slowly at the kitchen table.

"Oh, God." Daniel scrunched his face.

"Listen Daniel. Level with us. Are you telling the truth about our mom looking for us?" Lambert asked.

"Uh, well, uh...no. I made it up because I was mad at Eugene and you guys for making fun of me, and leaving me behind," Daniel explained.

"What about my old man and that cop Spike?" asked Jimmy.

"Nah, I made that up, too," Daniel admitted. "I made it all up."

"I ought to kick your—" Jimmy said as he swung at Daniel, but missed.

"Come on, guys!" Lambert interrupted.

"I can't believe you lied to us Daniel! I think I pooped my pants," said Chip.

"We can laugh later," Lambert said. "We've got to get on our bikes and go down to the river and look for Eugene. It's four-thirty and the sun will be coming up soon..."

"I don't have my bike, Lambert," Daniel said.

"It doesn't matter — you can use Eugene's. He won't care," explained Jimmy.

"How do you know?" asked Daniel.

"Think about it, dork," Jimmy smarted, "If he's dead it

won't matter." He then wheeled Eugene's bike away from the fence post. "Here, Daniel, it wasn't even locked."

"We've got to find him," Chip urged them on as they unlocked their bikes, "C'mon, hurry up." They pedaled out of the alley and headed for the river bridge. The flashing traffic signals bantered yellow and red back and forth along the boulevard while nighthawks darted overhead.

Lambert scanned the streets for police cars as he wondered when Eugene's mom would come down looking for him. He also began to yawn and felt tired. Chip and Jimmy weren't even keeping up with him and Daniel. Of course, Daniel had gotten in a bit of a nap while the rest of them were messing around down at the bridge.

"Come on, Jimmy! Chip! Pedal!" Lambert hollered back at the twosome, trailing behind in the morning fog. "We've got to search all along these tracks and under the bridge."

"And what if we don't find him there?" asked Daniel.

"If we don't find him there, then we'll follow the tracks to the south side of town!" Lambert directed.

"I hope we're the ones who find him," Chip said.

"Yeah we better do it now before somebody else finds him on their way to work," Daniel said.

"Shut up, Daniel," said Jimmy.

"Well, don't blame me. I wasn't with you when you helped kill him—"

"We didn't kill him!" Lambert shouted back, "We tried to tell him there was a train coming!"

"Daniel, it wasn't our fault! It wasn't even our idea to walk across the dang bridge!" Jimmy shouted.

"Just keep pedaling guys—" Daniel yelled.

"We're pedaling as fast as we can!" Chip hollered.

"We'll find him," Lambert promised.

By five a.m. they were down at the foot of the bridge. They

parked their bikes on the rocks and began climbing down the river bank.

"I can't go through all those weeds," Daniel complained. "I've got shorts on. There are spiders and snakes, poison ivy and thorn bushes in there."

"And skunks and possums," Jimmy laughed.

"Don't forget the ghost," Chip added in a raspy whisper.

Just as Jimmy and Daniel walked along the ties, calling out for Eugene, there was a sound from under the bridge.

"What's that?" Jimmy wailed.

A figure in white suddenly emerged. Daniel started running, grabbing Lambert and Chip, screaming aloud, "It's the ghost!"

The apparition of a gaunt visage surrounded by an off-white mantle startled them. Indeed Lambert feared that they had either roused the spirit of the railroad bridge or they were encountering Eugene's ghost – that is until he saw the familiar face of Scott Lawrence swathed in a dingy white blanket, emerging from a levee tomb like a specter of the shrouded Lazarus.

"Hey, I'm trying to sleep down here," Scott mumbled.

"We're looking for our friend," Lambert answered, relieved yet still frightened.

"Say, do any of you guys have enough money for a cup of coffee?"

"We might if you can you help us find our friend, Eugene," Jimmy said.

"I don't know him," Scott said before returning to his spot under the bridge.

"That danged bum scared the poop out of me," Jimmy said.

"Me, too," said Daniel.

"Let's keep looking guys," Chip said.

Chip and Lambert went under the bridge while Jimmy and Daniel walked out on it looking for Eugene or pieces of his clothing or anything which might be his or left of him.

"Eugene, we're back! Eugene, can you hear us?!" Lambert called out loudly, repeating himself several times.

"He ain't here, man. But look! Here's his shoe!" Daniel said as he held up a ripped black converse tennis shoe that he found on the trestle, "He's dead alright, but where's his body?!"

"Oh my God—" screamed Jimmy, "It's his—it's his shoe!! It's Eugene's tennis shoe!"

"How do you know?! Are you sure?!" Lambert pleaded, fearing the worst.

"Not exactly," Jimmy defended himself, "But how else could you rip a shoe unless you was getting run over by a train?!"

"That's not his shoe, you idiot!" Chip replied, sounding quite sure of what he said. "Look how small it is."

"Then where's his corpse?" asked Daniel.

"His what?" Jimmy puzzled.

"His *body*." Daniel lectured.

"Whatever — just look for hawks circling above. That's where you'll find his blood and guts and the rest of his body, but I'll bet his head came off," Jimmy snickered.

"Stop it," Lambert said, "Quit talking about his body! If you keep it up, it might come true. He's not here. Let's get back on our bikes and scan the tracks as far south as we can."

"All right, all right, but you best be thinking about what were going to do if we don't find him soon," Jimmy's voice quivered, "'cause his mom's going to miss him bad."

"I know, I know," Lambert answered, "I just hope we can find all of him," Lambert laughed. And everybody else laughed. It was a moment of comic relief that they all needed. It's not everyday that your friend gets smashed by a train. Meanwhile Lambert was racking his brain for ways to explain it to the police, to his mom and dad, and especially to Eugene's mom. Just the thought of it all made Lambert want to disappear.

They began the search by riding their bikes next to the tracks most of the way through town, but they never found anything except a torn red flannel shirt by Cardinal Creek. Jimmy cried aloud that it was Eugene's, but Eugene had been wearing a blue T-shirt. After much looking, there was still no sign of him anywhere. By the time the boys got to the cornfields south of town, they were physically and emotionally exhausted. Lambert believed that if anyone of them had started crying that morning, they all would have been bawling their eyes out – except maybe for Daniel.

The morning dampness glistened on their bike tires and the first streaks of the silent sun glowed over the horizon. They parked their bikes by the tracks next to the green fields and watched the sunrise burn off the morning dew. The red-winged blackbirds, mockingbirds, woodpeckers, crows, and cardinals sang their morning praise, songs of thanksgiving for having been preserved through the night and being allowed to live another day. So much for the birds; Eugene wasn't as fortunate.

After a few peaceful moments, seemingly free from worry, Lambert got back on his bike; Jimmy, Chip and Daniel did likewise. No one said anything to anyone as they rode back to the McChesney's camper. Lambert looked at his watch and it was six-thirty a.m.

Where is he?! Lambert kept asking himself. *O God, help us!* He prayed. Riding with the east to his back, the sun rose higher and higher behind him and it got warmer and warmer until he reached home. He and the others parked their bicycles near the trailer and Lambert suggested that they get their stuff and go in and call the police.

When Lambert opened the trailer door, Chip, Jimmy, and Daniel all followed in behind him. But as they got inside they were startled. There was someone sleeping in the trailer. They had left it unlocked while they were gone and someone had evidently made himself at home, possibly Scott Lawrence or some wino. Or was it Mr. or Mrs. McChesney?

All of a sudden the covers shifted and the person sat up in the bed. He pulled the covers from his face and began laughing.

It was Eugene Thomas. Eugene Thomas was alive!

"Ha! You guys! I fried your minds! I freaked you out!" Eugene gloated in laughter.

"Where in the heck have you been?!" Jimmy yelled, though obviously glad to see Eugene alive.

"Eugene, Where were you?!!" Lambert shouted, though relieved beyond belief.

"Eh, just as that train was going to hit me, I grabbed hold of one of the side railings on the bridge. I climbed up the side and hung on till the train went by. But when I saw all you guys looking for me, I climbed up on top of the bridge. Ha, you didn't say anything at first, but you thought I died. You thought I got run over! You thought I was dead. You thought I got killed. You thought I died! I was lying up there on that bridge listening to you guys calling for me like a danged dog! It was great! I got you guys good! Wait till I tell everybody at school!"

Jimmy, Daniel, Chip, and Lambert were furious. It was one of those rare times in a young man's life when he feels like hugging and kissing another guy and yet at the same time wanting to knock his teeth down his throat. Knowing Eugene, either action would have gotten any one of the boys killed. Lambert sighed, so thankful that he was alive.

All of them collapsed in their beds and they woke up around noon wringing wet with sweat. It felt like a hundred degrees in the trailer so they all grabbed their stuff and got out. Daniel started to walk home as Jimmy got on his bike to ride home.

"Where's *my* bike?" Eugene screamed. "Who took my bike?!"

"Daniel was riding it last night," Jimmy answered.

"Where'd you hide it, Danny boy?!" Eugene questioned him.

Daniel stuttered, "Uh, well, Jimmy gave it to me – we – we thought...."

"Jimmy, who told you he could use my bike?" Eugene

retorted.

"Well, we…we thought you were dead," stammered Jimmy.

"Yeah, but where's my dang bike?!" Eugene demanded.

"I don't know." Daniel answered. "When we got back this morning I leaned it up against the fence near everybody else's bike."

"Well, it's not here!"

"Then I guess somebody must've stolen it. You need to get yourself a combination lock like the rest of us. Sorry."

"Sorry's not good enough!! I'm going to kill you!" Eugene screamed as he started chasing Daniel out into oncoming traffic. Lambert, Chip and Jimmy all laughed as Eugene chased Daniel down the alley and across Bonaventure.

Poetic justice, Lambert supposed. He went to sleep knowing that they would all live to camp out yet another night.

Have courage. Go to sleep in peace. God is awake.
— Victor Hugo

BACON BREAKFAST

The following night the boys planned on staying in the trailer again, but this time they weren't going to the train bridge.

Eugene showed up at their house after dinner. "Guys, as I was riding my bike over by the animal hospital today I saw Sergeant Spike leaving his police dog, Goofy, at the vets. So I got a great idea. Let's go over to the payphone at the donut shop and call Spike."

Reluctantly Chip, Jimmy and Lambert went with him.

Eugene paged through the hanging phonebook, found the listing for Ronald Spike on Old Baxter Road, deposited a quarter, and dialed the number. When someone answered, Eugene asked in a high voice, "Is Ron Spike there?" He held the phone out for the others to hear.

"Yeah. This is him," the voice on the other end answered.

"Hey, this is the vet's office and we just wanted to call about your dog, Goofy." Eugene said in his best feminine voice.

"Yeah, what about him?'

"Well, we're just calling to let you know that we had him put to sleep this afternoon. You can pick up his collar and dog tag tonight—'"

At that the boys worked to stifle their laughter.

"Why'd you do that for?" Spike barked.

"Well, it seems after we declawed him and defanged him like you wanted us to do, his little heart just quit beating."

"He wasn't supposed to get defanged or declawed! He's a police dog, you idiot! You were supposed to give him his annual physical and rabies shots! You idiots! I was coming over to pick him up at seven-thirty!"

"Well, it'd sure be nice if you could, you know, come down here and get his carcass out of our office—he's starting to rot!"

"I'm coming down there right now!" Spike yelled into the

phone. "You'd better get yourself a good lawyer, you nincompoops!"

"Okay, we'll look forward to seeing you. Bye, bye." As soon as Eugene put the phone on its cradle they all began laughing. Lambert had to wipe tears from his eyes.

They walked back to Lambert and Chip's front porch and kept laughing about the phone call. About ten minutes later Spike sped by the house; his unmarked squad car's red dashboard light was flashing and his face was set like flint.

After some homerun derby and bike riding until dark, the guys were ready to camp. They had buttered popcorn and colas and root beer and played spades until midnight.

After one a.m., when the town grew quiet and the streets were unusually silent, Eugene took his blanket off his bed and carried it outside. The others followed him to see what he was doing. He then put it over his head and began running down the sidewalk. He called out, "Grab your blankets, guys! We'll run up and down the street with our blankets over our heads! We'll be ghosts!"

"Are you stupid?" Jimmy asked.

"Do it, weasel face," Eugene replied.

"Okay, okay, I was just joking," Jimmy said.

Lambert, Chip, and Jimmy got their blankets and put them over their heads and began running after Eugene down Bonaventure Avenue.

Eugene stopped at the corner and pondered, "Can you imagine, it's nearly two a.m. and there's no traffic."

"So what?" asked Jimmy, "It's the middle of the night."

"Duh – I know that," Eugene continued. "What I mean is that in the morning this street will be busy. It's one of the busiest in town. But, just think, right now we can lie down in the middle of the street."

Lambert knelt down to touch the pavement. It was cool. In

the quiet of the streetlight the Double Cola machine's compressor kicked on. They could hear the drone of highway traffic over a mile and a half away while some night hawks flitted about, calling out to one another, as a whippoorwill sang on repeatedly. Then Eugene took his blanket and fluffed it out on the street and lay on it.

"C'mon, guys! This is cool!" Eugene said as he stared into the sky.

"Are you loco, dude?" asked Chip.

"No. Just do it. It'll be something you can tell everybody," Eugene persisted.

"The cops will see us!" warned Jimmy, "Either that, or else you'll really get killed this time."

"Man, would you just quit worrying about everything!" said Eugene as he stretched out in the middle of the street, "Don't worry about it—"

"Aw, yeah, that's easy for you to say. You're not the one with an old man who totes around a shotgun—" Jimmy explained.

"Yeah, I don't even have an old man," Eugene boasted, "*I'm* the old man of my house!"

"What happened to your dad, Eugene?" Jimmy inquired.

Eugene paused and looked at Lambert.

"C'mon, guys, lay down here in the street!" Eugene spoke again, evading the question. One by one they reluctantly lay down on their blankets in the street.

"Yeah, when I was born," Eugene continued, "my ol' man took one look at me and said 'he's one mean son of a butcher!' Then he took off."

"Where is he now?" Lambert asked.

"In jail," Jimmy interrupted, "because when you were born he tried to smother you when he saw how ugly you was!"

"Shut up!" shouted Eugene.

"Really, Eugene, where is your dad?" Chip asked.

"I don't know," Eugene answered softly. "I don't know. Just leave me alone, all right." They respected Eugene for his honesty as they lay there looking up, gazing at the stars and the crescent moon. They were silent for about a minute.

"Jimmy?" Chip spoke up, displacing the quiet.

"Yeah," he answered.

"You ever miss your mom?" Chip asked Jimmy.

"Yeah. Sometimes. I really don't remember her though. I don't know why." Jimmy answered.

"How's come?" Chip asked.

"I don't know. It's weird. Sometimes I can't even remember what she looked like or what her voice sounded like," answered Jimmy.

None of them quite knew how to respond to Jimmy or talk to him about his mother's death. It had only been about a year since she died.

"Where do you think she went, man?" asked Jimmy.

"What do you mean?" Eugene asked. "She died."

"Yeah, but I mean, you know, you think she went to heaven or hell?" Jimmy continued.

"Who knows? Who cares? She's dead, man. She's dead and gone. That's it. You live and then you die," Eugene explained.

"That's a heck of a thing to say, Eugene," Jimmy shouted.

"Eugene, don't you believe in God?" Lambert spoke up.

"No. You can't prove there's a God, Lambert," Eugene answered.

"Well, you can't prove there's not a God," Lambert argued. "And what about heaven? Don't you want to go to heaven?"

"No, 'cause it ain't there," he shot back.

"Why do you say that?"

"You and Chip are Catholics, aren't you—some weird stuff, man."

"What do you mean by that?" Lambert asked, offended.

"Well, for one thing, you can't have sex till you're married and you got to go to Church all the time," Eugene elaborated.

"But that's the way it's supposed to be," Lambert hammered back.

Jimmy entered the conversation, "Eugene, I ain't Catholic. Well, I was baptized one, but I don't go to Church or anything like that, but you are supposed to wait till you're married before you—"

"You guys don't have any fun," Eugene said in a huff.

"I think we do a pretty good job of it.   I   mean,   look, we're out here lying in the middle of the street, aren't we?" Lambert said.

"Yeah, but I'm talking about making out with girls," Eugene said.

"Making out what?" asked Chip.

"Why would I want to do that?" Jimmy asked.

"Yeah, I'm not a girl," Chip echoed the point.

Lambert knew what Eugene was getting at.

"Ha, you guys are idiots!" Eugene shook his head. "Lambert, what do you say we go over to *the Pancake Palace* and try to pick up a couple of chicks—maybe we could French kiss 'em."

"What?" asked Chip, looking at Eugene.

"When you kiss a girl and you touch your tongues together 'n stuff—" Eugene described the kiss.

"Gross!" said Chip.

"That's sick! That's like letting a dog lick you," Jimmy added, turning to look at Eugene.

"You two must be queer or something—" Eugene said.

"We ain't queer, man!" yelled Chip.

"I ain't a queer, Eugene—" Jimmy snapped, "Takes one to know one—"

"Hey, if it feels good, do it," replied Eugene.

Lambert stood with his blanket draped over his shoulders and looked at Chip, Jimmy, and Eugene lying in the street as he thought of a way to respond to Eugene's philosophy on pleasure.

Suddenly Chip yelled, "Truck!"

A truck's engine revved and the tires sang on the pavement. The boys jerked towards the stoplight by the Purple Finch and saw a delivery truck coming.

"Get up! Get up!" Lambert cried.

"You're on my blanket, Dip!" Jimmy hollered at Eugene. Eugene, Jimmy, and Chip were all fighting to get to their feet and get their legs unwrapped from the blankets, which were twisted every which way. They wrestled with the blankets as they staggered to their feet and made it over to the curb. They collapsed on the grass as the truck drove by. The driver tooted his horn as he roared by them.

They sat on the front steps for nearly a quarter hour just watching what was going on over at *the Pancake Palace*.

"What would happen if one of us were to go over there and order a coke-to-go or something?" Chip asked. "Sure would be nice to have some French fries or a burger."

"Or maybe some blueberry waffles," longed Jimmy.

"We ain't got no time for no waffles, dummy!" Eugene blasted.

"What're you going to order, Eugene? Tongue?" asked Jimmy.

At that Eugene lunged at Jimmy and held his face to the ground and said, "You're going to eat dirt if you don't shut your fat mouth!"

"I'd rather eat grass!" choked Jimmy.

"I'd rather *smoke* it," Eugene bragged.

"I'm going to get my dad to kick your butt!" Jimmy threatened.

"Bring him on! I can take him out. He'd have a heart attack before I'd even get to throw a punch!" Eugene continued to rough-house Jimmy, "He'd drop dead just knowing I was going to kick his arse!"

"No, he'd die, 'cause you're so danged ugly—" said Jimmy as he managed to squeeze it out of his mouth while Eugene pushed his face harder into the lawn.

"C'mon, Eugene. Stop it! He's just joking," Lambert pleaded.

"Okay, I'll let you live this time, bub!" said Eugene as he pulled Jimmy up by the hair and threw him to the side.

"So you think you can take my old man, do ya?" Jimmy started right back up again.

"Yeah. I could whoop him one-handed and blindfolded!" Eugene said as he strutted away, puffing out his chest.

At that their attention focused on the street where a slow moving police car came cruising by. It was none other than officer Spike with his canine partner, Goofy. No one moved.

Spike slowly drove by and glared at Eugene. His window was rolled down, his head cocked back, a cigarette clenched between his teeth, and his left hand resting in the open window aiming his spotlight on him. Goofy was standing up in the back seat sticking his head out the back window, panting, his tongue hanging out of his head. As his car rolled by, Spike put his hand to his mouth and took a drag off his cigarette and exhaled the smoke through his nose.

Then he stopped his squad car in the middle of the street, directly across from the McChesney's house, kicked his door open, stretched out of the car, and stood in the street. He continued to point his spotlight at Eugene. "Thomas? Eugene Thomas. I'm watching you. And Goofy here's got a score to settle with you too." Taking the nearly finished lit cigarette from his mouth, he flicked it halfway across the street and said with a smile, "You'd best be good little boys. All of you. Or I guarantee you, I'll take y'all downtown." He slowly got back in his car, pointing at them all. "No more high jinks, monkeyshines or tomfoolery, you hear?" He took out another cigarette from his shirt pocket and lit it up. Then he reached around and gave

Goofy a doggie biscuit before he turned his spotlight off and sped away, with a squeal of his tires.

As he got about a half-block away Eugene jumped in the street and yelled, "Pig! Come on back here, I'll turn that dumb dog of yours into Goofy-burgers! I'll show you what a real man is!" Eugene turned towards the boys and said, "Jerk, man. He's a jerk. I think he likes to pick on me because I don't got an old man—probably wants to go out with my mom. He called her up last year and told her he could arrange to keep me out of trouble. She hung up on him."

Chip changed the subject and said, "Hey, let's cook some bacon!"

"Yeah, I'm hungry," said Jimmy.

"You're always hungry, fatso," said Eugene.

"Shut up, you orangutan" laughed Jimmy.

Lambert, Jimmy, and Chip went back to the trailer. Jimmy found the lighter fluid; Lambert brought the bacon from the camper fridge; and Chip set up his dad's portable grill. Chip put the grill in the middle of the yard as Jimmy soaked the lumps of charcoal in the starter fluid. Chip struck the match and it ignited in a huge fireball. Lambert and Chip ran from the blaze.

"Aw, man! Chip screamed, "I singed my face! You dumb-head! How much of that stuff did you use, Jimmy?!"

"Uh, I don't 'member. I just squirted it in the grill," Jimmy explained.

Eugene and Lambert laughed.

"Well, where's the bacon?" asked Chip.

"I got it." Lambert said as he brought it out of the cooler and walked it over to the grill.

"Put it on the grill," Jimmy said.

Lambert carefully placed them on the grill, "Here's eight pieces—that's two a piece."

"Okay. Just let 'em cook," said Chip.

But after about a minute, Jimmy was becoming impatient,

and said, "I don't see any flames. It ain't cooking."

"Yeah it is. The charcoal's hot," Lambert said.

"It'll cook if you got hot lumps of charcoal," explained Eugene.

"No it ain't. Look—" Jimmy argued.

"You soaked the charcoal—just leave it alone! Don't put anymore of that lighter fluid on it—" Eugene countered.

"No! Jimmy, don't!!" Chip yelled as Jimmy was going for the can of lighter fluid.

"Here—we got to get that fire 'goin'!" Jimmy fought past Lambert and Chip.

They yelled for Jimmy not to put anymore lighter fluid on the fire. Eugene tried to wrestle the can away from him, but Jimmy poured it on the grill anyway. Unfortunately it gushed forth out of the can and went all over the top of the grill—right on the bacon and instantly there was a huge rush of sound and the yard and trees lit up in red and yellow as a fireball rolled off the top of the grill. Eugene and Jimmy jumped away, hitting the ground. The sky was bright orange and a cloud of smoke hovered above the yard.

Eugene punched Jimmy in the gut. "What're you tryin' to do—get us killed?! We could've all been burnt, that can could've exploded, you dumb ox!"

"Oooh! My stomach—I think you ruptured my appendix—"

"That ain't all I'm going to rupture," Eugene fired back.

"No, my Dad says you can kill a guy hitting him in the gut like that! Man! I can't breathe!" Jimmy moaned.

"If you couldn't breathe, you wouldn't be whining!" Eugene assured Jimmy.

Lambert and Chip were distracted from the ruckus when a car pulled over to the curb in front of their house. It was a county sheriff's car and there were two officers inside. Loud garbled voices came from their two-way radio.

One of the officers waved Lambert over. "Boys—what in the

blazes are you doing?"

None of them answered as they stood motionless, between the blazing grill and the idling squad car. Silence ensued until Lambert nervously answered, "Uh, well, uh—we're cooking ourselves some breakfast. Bacon. A guy's got to eat, you know."

"Uh, huh. Well, did you boys plan on burning down your neighborhood?" asked the cop on the passenger side, with a bit of a laugh in his voice.

"Uh, no, not really. We've been camping out."

"Well," the policeman replied, "You ought to go to a campground for that! You better be careful and go get some sleep, and you ought to be glad Sergeant Spike didn't see you guys do that trick with the fire. The city cops are watching you guys." It was a brief moment of comic relief as the cops themselves snickered. "We saw it while we were having coffee at the Pancake Palace," the police officer added. Lambert laughed under his breath.

"Oh, uh, Yeah—well, thanks. Goodnight officers." Lambert stammered out as they drove away. Eugene, Jimmy, and Chip didn't say anything as Lambert walked back to the grill. He looked at the bacon and it looked like it was ready. Each of them grabbed a couple of slices and began to eat it.

"Jimmy, it tastes like lighter fluid!" Eugene shouted.

"That's because he soaked the bacon in it," Chip said, shaking his head.

They ate it anyway.

"You know," Eugene said, "with as many cops around here, we could have lots of bacon."

They all laughed. Afterwards they got inside the camper and fell asleep.

When Lambert told his mother the next morning that he and Chip had eaten bacon marinated in charcoal lighter fluid she said that they'd probably develop some type of stomach cancer.

That was something to look forward to.

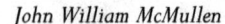

What's another word for Thesaurus?

HOLYDAYS & HOLIDAYS

The next night Lambert and the others were out in the trailer again, but exactly how much time they would spend inside the trailer, or how much time they would spend sleeping was questionable. The moon was full and Lambert felt as if its gravitational pull was tugging on his forehead.

Sometime after ten o'clock, Eugene and Jimmy were embroiled in a conversation about God.

"Well, Jimmy, if there's a God, how's come you don't go to church like Lambert and Chip?"

"Because we just don't go all the time. Me and my dad always go to the Baptist church at Christmas, and Easter sometimes, but church is long and boring," Jimmy explained.

"Yeah, Jimmy," Lambert entered the conversation, "but Christmas and Easter are the longest services of the whole year. So if you're only going to go twice a year, go during the summer or something. Or pick a church that doesn't have air-conditioning. They'll get you in and out in a half an hour."

"You think?" Jimmy asked.

"I don't know." Lambert laughed.

"Okay, then tell me this one, guys," Eugene continued his ponderings. "Who made God?"

"But," Lambert began, "God didn't, or, God isn't...God wasn't created. He's always been."

"That don't make sense," Eugene retorted.

"Really?" Lambert asked. "Then, where did the earth and the moon and the sun and the stars come from?"

"They're just billions of years old," Eugene answered.

"Yeah, but where'd they come from?" Lambert asked.

"Who knows? They've always been; it's always been. You know – evolution."

"So the universe has always been?"

"Yeah."

"Well, then…if…that's the reason, *that* doesn't make any sense!"

"What do you mean? Why not?"

"If God couldn't have always been, then how can you say that about the universe."

"I don't know. This is different. You can see the universe and stuff. God's like…God's like Santa Claus–"

"What?" Lambert exclaimed.

"Yeah. Your Mom and Dad lied to you guys about Santa Claus to get you to keep your room clean and make you mind them. So you did. Then when he'd come every year you thought it was because you were good–"

"How the——" Lambert started to speak.

"Wait, let me finish. You guys obeyed and you got some nice stuff at Christmas. But you finally figured out Santa was fake and you stopped worrying about being bad and not getting Christmas presents and stuff."

"Yeah, well, I don't know," Lambert said softly.

"Eugene's a philosopher over here," cracked Jimmy.

"No I ain't——I'm just telling you the truth," Eugene shot back.

"Well, then," Lambert continued, "Eugene, why do we exist?"

"Are you for real? Jimmy and Chip, close your ears. I've got to explain the birds and the bees to Lambert."

"Ha, ha," Jimmy rolled his eyes at Eugene.

"No, Eugene," Lambert replied. "I'm not talking about *how* human beings are conceived. I'm asking why any of us is here at all?"

"Beats me, but as long as I'm here I'm going to get whatever I can get away with."

"So you don't think there might be a God?"

"No."

"You don't even think there *could be* a God?"

"Nah. I mean, look at it. If everybody lied to us about Santa Claus, then what else were they lying to us about, huh?"

"Well, God isn't Santa Claus. There really was a Saint Nicholas. He was a bishop in the early Church—" Lambert started to explain before being interrupted again.

"Yeah, yeah, but you see some people like that Saint Nick and that pope guy and all those other guys dressed in those funny little dresses—"

"They're called cassocks," Lambert interrupted.

"Eh, whatever," continued Eugene, "but they look like long dresses. Anyway, all those old people got together a long, long time ago and came up with an idea about a God and stuff—like the Ten Commandments—so they could scare you, and get you so you couldn't have any fun and then they'd make money off of you too, getting you to go to church every Sunday."

"Who's been teaching you that rubbish?" Lambert asked.

"Mrs. Hunter at school—and it ain't rubbish!"

"Well, that's not true," Lambert argued.

"Yeah, it is!"

"Well, then she must be an atheist"

"No she's not, she's nothing—she doesn't go to church or anything. She doesn't even believe in God."

"That's what I mean," Lambert sighed. "An atheist doesn't believe in God."

"Oh."

"Well, I don't have her for class," Jimmy spoke up again, "but my teacher believes in God and we still do the 'pledge of allegiance'."

"Oh, we do it, too, but we don't say that 'Under God' thing. We leave that out of it," Eugene said.

"Oh, and I'll bet Mrs. Hunter's behind that, too," Lambert suggested.

"Sort of – she let our class decide whether we'd say it or

not," Eugene explained.

"Don't you ever pray?" Chip asked.

"No. Why would I want to do that? Prayer is a waste of time since there's no god. Besides, prayer distracts you from 'real life'."

"Did you ever believe in God?" Lambert inquired.

"Maybe when I was little."

"Well, then why don't you still believe?"

"I don't need to. I grew up. When will you?"

"Did you believe in Santa Claus when you were a kid?"

"Not really. I knew it was all a lie when we'd go to the department store and there'd always be a different Santa. And then when I'd ask him to bring me stuff, they'd always say, 'I'll see what I can do', or 'I'll have to check with my elves'. Other kids didn't hear that. Made me think I was bad. Then when Christmas would get here I didn't get diddlysquat. But when I'd go back to school all the other kids would be bragging how Santa brought them all kinds of toys and new clothes.

"Me and the black kids had it all figured out. Santa was only for rich white kids. C'mon, did you ever see a black Santa? It made my black friends feel like dog dung. It's all a bunch a lies, man. Look, my mom told me one night after she'd been to a Christmas party or something—she didn't want me to get my hopes up for nothing. I remember that. And it's that way with God, too."

"That's sad, but believing in God isn't like believing in Santa Claus," Lambert replied.

"I say it is."

"Well, you can believe what you want, Eugene, but until you can explain how the universe got here, I'll go on believing in God."

"Yeah, did Santa have the universe in his toy bag, 'Gene?" Jimmy blurted out.

"Aw, shut up brainless! I didn't see you having anything to

say. You probably don't even know why you go to Church on Christmas!" said Eugene.

"Do, too!" Jimmy emphatically replied.

"Jimmy still believes the Easter Bunny lays plastic colored eggs!" Eugene joked.

"Do not!" Jimmy yelled out.

"Guys," Chip entered in, "Did you know that if you take the letters that spell Santa and rearrange them you can spell Satan?!"

"Ssshhhh! Jimmy still believes in Sanni' Claus, too. Better not let him find out Santa is Satan!" laughed Eugene.

"Hey, guys," Chip said, "any of you got some matches?"

"Why?" asked Eugene.

"'Cause I still got about a brick and a half of firecrackers left over from the fourth of July."

"No way?!" Eugene exclaimed as only Eugene could when it came to talk of fireworks. "I got a great idea."

"What's that?" Chip asked.

"Since we don't have any bottle rockets left, we could take the firecrackers and light them on the steps of the police station," Eugene plotted. "That'll bring Officer Spike around, won't it?"

"Yeah," Lambert replied. "That'll do it."

"I miss the old dude and his doggie!" Eugene said, mockingly wiping away tears. "Let's go."

"What!" Lambert exclaimed. "No way! It's too dangerous."

"Don't worry about it, Lambers," Eugene reassured him. "This'll be too cool! If it goes down we'll say it was my idea, but if we get caught it'll be all Jimmy's fault, ha ha!"

"I ain't taking all the blame!" Jimmy whined. "My dad will kill me dead!"

"Is that a promise? I'd like to help him," laughed Eugene. Lambert and Chip laughed too.

"Okay guys, let's call Spike before we go do it," Eugene announced. "Lambert, come with me and we'll go call Goofy's boy!"

"No! They can trace those phone calls!" Lambert implored.

"Okay. Well, then you got a handkerchief?" Eugene asked.

Never being without his trusty hanky, Lambert replied, "Uh, Yeah. Why?"

"I need one," said Eugene.

"Okay. Here," Lambert pulled it from his front left pocket and handed it to him.

"Good. Now we won't leave our fingerprints on the phone," smiled Eugene. "Now let's go!" Eugene yelled as he grabbed Lambert's arm.

"Go ahead and do it, Lambie," Jimmy encouraged him while Chip giggled with excitement. Before Lambert could argue any further, Eugene had him in tow. He and Eugene looked both ways down the silent street carefully watching for oncoming cars and people as they ran across to the parking lot of The Burger Place where the payphone stood.

Eugene opened the door to the phone booth and both of them got inside. Eugene took the receiver off the hook, placed the handkerchief over the microphone, and dialed the number to the police department. Lambert looked around for cop cars as Eugene held the phone away from his ear so that they both could hear the phone ring.

After four rings a woman answered, "Preston Point City Police Department..."

"Uh, Yeah," Eugene began in a deep voice, "Is officer Spike there?"

"Sergeant Spike's out on patrol this morning," the female dispatcher replied.

"Good. You tell him that Big Ed's going to get him tonight." Eugene paused a second or two in order to catch his breath, holding in a laugh.

He smiled at Lambert as the dispatcher asked, "What? Is this a serious call? Who's Big Ed?"

"Yeah, I'm serious. You just let ol' Spikey know that we're coming for him and his puny puppy! He'll know who it is. Bye, bye!" Eugene slammed the phone down and he fought Lambert to get out of the booth first. They ran all the way back to the trailer. Lambert's stomach was in knots.

"Eugene threatened – Eugene threatened Spike's life!" Lambert gasped out.

"Ha! The lady at the police station was freaking out, man!" Eugene exulted without a trace of worry or fear in what he had just done.

"You think they were able to trace the call?!" Lambert asked.

"It don't matter," said Eugene, "and even if they did, they won't find out who called 'em."

"Are you sure?" asked Jimmy.

"I'm sure. Now let's go light those firecrackers. Lambert, you got the matches?"

"Uh, Yeah—I think," Lambert sheepishly said. He began opening and closing the trailer's kitchen drawers in his search until he found some. Lambert took a matchbook out of the knife and fork drawer and Eugene grabbed it out of his hand. Then they all bailed out the door and headed towards the police station. They walked down the sidewalk on most streets; either they were getting bolder or dumber. They were about halfway there when some dogs started barking. For about a two block stretch everywhere there were dogs barking, screeching, and howling. Porch lights started coming on and Lambert thought the worst.

Jimmy looked as if he was experiencing a spasm, his chin quivering as he breathed out in a hiss, "Cops, man! My dad, my dad! Spike will sic Goofy on us! We should've never come!"

"Shut up!!" said Eugene with anger in his eyes, "Listen!"

Lambert thought Eugene was part Indian because he could hear everything long before any of the others heard anything. Creeping along in front of them was a black and white squad car, car number forty-four, coming down the alley where all the dogs were barking.

"Quick, hide!" Lambert said as he, Jimmy and Chip dove between two parked cars while Eugene crawled underneath one of them – an old Grey mercury – and lay flat on his stomach. The cop car exited the alley and drove away in the opposite direction. Lambert, Jimmy, and Chip got up as soon as the cop was up the street. Eugene came up out from under the Mercury on the side of the curb. When he stood up he had a huge blob of oil and grease on the front of his T-shirt. He felt it on his stomach and he said, "Gross!" Then he peeled off his shirt, stuck one end of it in his back pocket, and looked at Jimmy, "What're you starin' at, my tits?"

"I ain't looking at your chest, Eugene!" Jimmy whined back.

"Yeah you are. You're queer for me," the bare-chested Eugene chuckled and shook his head. Then he straightened with a serious look across his face. "Let's go."

The pyrotechnic mission was still clear in his mind.

"Let's go back, guys," Jimmy begged. "The cops will catch us!"

"Yeah. Chip, you better take the little baby Jimmy back to the camper and tuck him in under the covers so he'll be all safe and snuggly! Eugene said sweetly.

"I ain't no baby, you big goof!" Jimmy shot back. "I ought to take you out."

"You and what army? Oh, like I'm so scared," mocked Eugene. "Now, go on. Get going. You and Chip wait back at the trailer for us. Lambert and I'll go set these firecrackers off ourselves!" Lambert was flattered that Eugene wanted him to go with him, even though he was so scared he thought he was about to wet his pants.

Eugene stood there in the dim street light, shirtless, holding the explosives. Rarely, if ever, did Lambert go without a shirt, but Eugene didn't seem to notice any difference. He then handed Lambert the matches and they were well on their way.

Lambert prayed that they wouldn't get caught.

In the thick humid midnight air, a tavern's neon sign flickered and hummed; a garbage truck banged and clanked a dumpster; a hot-rodder burnt rubber along the main drag; crickets chirped; and cicadas whined. In the moonlight one large oak tree stood out. As Lambert walked under the tree it looked like a gigantic crucifix; the trunk's twining resembled the sinews of the corpus of Christ. As he walked under it, the image hauntingly bore a resemblance to a Renaissance sculpture, each angle revealing more detail, open to interpretation.

The two wound their way through unfamiliar alleys and neighborhoods until they got downtown about a block away from the police station. Lambert's lower jaw felt numb as he stuck his head out from behind a service station and a row of trash cans in a darkened alley.

"There it is," whispered Eugene, as he handed Lambert a brick. "Now, you stay here while I go do it! If you see anybody coming, take this brick and rap it against one of the trash cans to get my attention."

Thank God, Lambert said to himself. He thought Eugene had wanted him to actually be the one to light the firecrackers.

"When I go to light them, you start running like crazy, man," Eugene continued, "'Cause I'll probably pass you up once I catch up with you."

"Okay, but don't leave me behind," Lambert pleaded.

"I won't," Eugene promised as he scooted across the street. He stayed close to the walls of the jail and crawled up the stairway near the front door.

As Lambert stood in the silent darkness watching him it seemed like the whole city was holding its breath. Lambert didn't hear anything: no cars, no trains, nothing, not anything, anywhere. Everything was quiet. Too quiet. Then Lambert saw a flash of light appear in Eugene's hand. His face lit up, bathed in a glow of light. Then Eugene's mouth opened wide in a loud "RUN!" as he jumped up and leapt down the stairway with great strides. Sprinting across the street he tripped and tumbled in the street, his limbs flailing, but cat-like he landed back upright on his feet continuing his mad dash.

The firecrackers began exploding loudly, shattering the silence. Eugene had lit all of them—over two hundred. The feeling of accomplishment that rushed through his body from head to toe caused Lambert to stand still and glory in this moment of stupidity even though he knew that the cops would be descending on the jail in a matter of moments.

Eugene looked at Lambert wild-eyed and yelled, "Go! Go! Go!" Lambert began running and the firecrackers kept banging. Eugene caught up with him in the next block. But they stopped dead in their tracks when a shrill police siren began to wail loudly. It was getting closer and closer. Lambert thought of Chip and Jimmy. Did they get back okay? Or did Spike catch them and make them tell him where he and Eugene were? Lambert imagined that the cops traced the phone call to that phone booth and the cops were waiting for them in the trailer.

Lambert turned and saw a black and white, more of a gray streak, hurtling down the street towards the police station and Eugene turned around, running backwards, and jumped in the air, and gave Lambert a 'high five', "Yeah, baby! We freaked 'em out, man! They're calling for back-up!" The two continued running as fast as they could.

When they got to the side street between the trailer and 'no man 's land' they saw another police car parked across the street from *the Pancake Palace*. Together they decided, without thinking, to go for it. Bolting across Second Avenue, they carefully made their way up the last two alleys to their block, only encountering one barking dog before getting to the end of the last alley where they had to jump over some shrubs and hide. Because, there, just less than one city block separating them from freedom, was yet still another police car in the middle of the street with its engine running and the headlights on. Lambert couldn't see which car it was, but if it was car seventy-seven then they were all in big trouble.

Eugene turned to Lambert and asked in a whisper, "Is it Spike?" But before Lambert could answer they heard a dog bark. And then a voice.

"It's okay, Goofy," Spike's voice echoed off the pavement. "I'll let you out in just a second." But Goofy kept barking, louder and louder.

Oh, my God. I'm dead. Life's sure been nice, and the firecracker thing was cool, but this is not good, Lambert thought to himself. He could feel his heart thumping in his chest as he tried to catch his breath. He found himself making incredible wagers with God, *Oh, Lord, if I get out of this mess, then I'll help mom clean the house*, and other such bargains and empty promises of the same ridiculous nature freely flowed.

Eugene breathed out, "Lambert, Goofy's barkin' because of us. Once Spike opens that door and lets him out, he'll come right over to us and then we're dead meat, man. Dead meat."

"Oh, scheis," Lambert whispered.

"Scheis is right," he replied, "Now, Lamb, you see those empty beer bottles over there by that trash can?"

"Yeah. Why?"

"Go get a couple of 'em and bring 'em here."

"No way."

"Yeah. You got to do it, Lammers."

"Why? Why me? You do it."

"You're smaller."

"Why do you need them?"

"You do want to get out of here don't you?"

"Yeah."

"We're going to throw the bottles in the middle of the street so it will distract Spike and Goofy. They'll head for the breaking glass and when they do, we'll run down to the other end of the alley. They'll never see us. Easy as pie."

"This better work."

"You got a better idea?"

"Let me think."

"Just get going before Goofy finds us."

"Okay. Hang on." Lambert reluctantly crawled over to the trash pit and grabbed two of the empty brown beer bottles. As he made his way back to Eugene, he could see Spike heading for his police car.

"Here I come, Goof. I'll let you out," Spike said.

Lambert began to pray again, this time beseeching the intercession of the Virgin Mary.

Eugene grabbed him and said, "Stand up, and on a count of three throw it as hard as you can out that way, so it'll land on the sidewalk out front. As soon as the glass breaks they'll start heading that way and that's when we'll run back to your house!"

"Okay."

"One-two-three-heave!" They threw the bottles and they shattered in the street. Spike was letting Goofy out of the car just as the glass started breaking so he and the dog ran towards the sound while Lambert and Eugene jumped across the shrubs, raced through the gravel, and darted down the alley to the trailer. When they got there Eugene jerked the trailer door open and he and Lambert jumped inside. Chip and Jimmy were wide awake. Jimmy said in a loud voice, "It was great! You could hear firecrackers everywhere!"

"Yeah," Lambert panted out, catching his breath.

"That was close," sighed Eugene, with a look of relief.

"Shut up, guys!" Jimmy said with a terrified look on his face, "Here comes a car."

Lambert reached over and pulled the curtain to the side; all four of them saw it at the same time—car seventy-seven—in the alley, next to Mr. McChesney's station wagon.

Goofy was barking but, as if a miracle, Spike just kept driving down the alley.

Lambert thought that was enough excitement for one night. After he and Eugene told Chip and Jimmy everything from the firecrackers at the jailhouse to the broken beer bottles, they collapsed after an hour or so and slept till noon the next day.

Observe everything, overlook a lot, correct a little.
— Blessed Pope John XXIII

CLOSE ENCOUNTERS IN THE RAIL YARD

The moon was still full or at least almost as full as last night's moon. Shortly before ten o'clock Daniel's mom dropped him off so he could spend another night with his cousins.

"Daniel, last night we bombed the police station with firecrackers!" Eugene boasted.

"No way?!" And together Jimmy and Chip went on to describe how Eugene and Lambert got chased by the cops.

The boys walked down Sixth Avenue. Lots of teenagers were still out cruising the strip, so the five weren't in much danger of getting caught for breaking curfew. They stopped at the Seven Eleven and bought some Double Cola and chocolate bars before heading back to the trailer. Even though they didn't sleep the night before, nothing would or could stop them now. They'd be up all night bouncing off the walls.

Now the guys were ready to begin another night of fun and games—this time five strong. And Daniel had a surprise for them all.

Lambert and Daniel wanted to go to the train depot. Eugene couldn't understand why anyone would want to go down to an old depot and watch trains at night. Lambert couldn't really explain it, either. It just was.

At the Union Depot, trains abounded. The air was perfumed with the scent of diesel fuel, the locomotives coughing up clouds of acrid smoke, the grinding and whining of the engines, their gnashing wheels upon the pinging, popping, and singing rails and the creaking crossties under the crushing weight of the train and the chafing grate of the roadbed of rocks, the knell of the engine's bells and clamor of horns, the thump, rattle, squeak, and screech of the rolling freight cars, and the clank and clash, clack and clatter, and jangle of the wheels over the junction of rails was unparalleled in excitement and power.

Three passenger trains still stopped at Preston Point in the late 1960s, but by 1973 passenger service came to an end.

The din of the night freight trains rumbling through town, the switch engines in the railroad yards, the crash of couplers and hissing air brakes, the sight of a brakemen swinging their lanterns, (a vanishing breed of men), the diesel engine's clanging bell and bold horn, flashing red wig-wag lights, and the toll of crossing gate bells, and the lingering scent of coal cinders among the ballast from yesteryear charged the heavy, humid night air with an energy all its own.

To Lambert there was nothing like the vitality of a train horn, clatter of freight cars, rumble of wheels, and undulating screech of rails heralding a train's passage through town. It could be that since his grandpa and dad both worked for the railroad, Lambert may have been born with memory genes. He'd always loved trains and he couldn't remember not longing to watch the trains come through town and to lie in bed and listen to the mournful whistles and the droning deafening diesel horns singing in the night. Whatever it was, there was something mystical, magical, and spiritual about waiting for trains and watching them go by.

As Lambert and Eugene started to cross the street and leave for the railroad yards, Daniel said, "Hey, guys, wait up!"

"What is it now, are you chicken?" Eugene asked.

"I ain't chicken! Check this out..." said Daniel as he slowly pulled his T-shirt up above his belt. He unveiled a secret weapon in their siege upon Officer Spike. Under his shirt, strapped to his belt, was a new, hand-held pocket police scanner. All of them watched as four flashing red lights went back and forth on his radio that looked like a walkie-talkie.

"What's that?" Eugene asked.

"It's a scanner," Daniel replied, "my grandma bought it for me on my birthday!"

"What's it do?" Eugene asked.

"It'll tell us where the cops and the fire department are going and stuff."

"Cool!" Eugene lit up with a big smile.

"Where'd she get it?" asked Jimmy.

"At the electronic store."

"How can you understand what they're saying-isn't it all in code?" asked Jimmy.

"Lambert, Chip, and I know all the codes," explained Daniel.

"Guys, how's come you know the police codes?" Eugene asked.

"Our mom has a scanner," Chip answered.

Suddenly Daniel's scanner squelched loudly.

"Listen—it's a call for car seventy-seven," Daniel said.

"That's Spike's car!" Chip said with a mouthful of chocolate and peanuts.

"I'll bet Goofy's with him," Lambert rejoined as he sipped his cola.

"Oh, Gawd," Jimmy exclaimed.

"Where they, going? Eugene asked.

The radio squawked and a voice came across, "Car seventy-seven — meet the lady at 2608 Bonaventure Boulevard in reference to a burglar."

Then a second or two later a voice boomed out, breaking the silence as a single red light burned steadily on the radio fastened to Daniel's belt. "Headquarters — Car seventy-seven's en route!"

"Car seventy-seven. Zero hundred hours, fifty-three minutes."

"That's Spike, man!" Lambert said loudly.

"Oh Gawd, if he's out tonight—then we'd better not fart around and do anything stupid, man." Jimmy exclaimed.

"Well, you can go back and stay in the trailer and hide all night, but the rest of us are going to raise Cain!" Eugene countered as he finished off his candy bar.

"Yeah——" said Daniel, trying to act as big and as tough as Eugene.

"Don't push it, Danny boy," Eugene interrupted, "you're just lucky I'm going to let you stay in the McChesney's trailer."

"I did bring my scanner over——" Daniel attempted to justify his presence.

"Okay, okay, that's good," said Eugene. "Let's go find Sonny Sage."

"Aw, man, that guy's bats," said Chip.

"No telling what he would do," Jimmy said. "Let's get Raymond."

"You mean Frankenstein from hell?" asked Chip.

Daniel, looking puzzled asked, "Who's that?"

"Raymond Wilson," Jimmy answered. "He's really messed up."

"Yeah, nuttier than the dude from *One Flew Over The Cuckoo's Nest*——" Chip added.

"No way! You guys are just trying to freak me out – Lambert tell 'em I know they're making this stuff up," Daniel replied as he slurped his cola.

"No we're not, Daniel. He really is a mental case." Lambert said. "Look——the guy spent a couple of years in a mental hospital."

"Why? What's wrong with him?" Daniel asked.

"He was in the Vietnam War and he never got over it. I guess he hasn't been right since," Lambert explained.

"What do you mean? What happened to him?" Daniel persisted.

"We don't know," Lambert explained. "He has flashbacks and stuff. Sometimes he thinks he's still in Vietnam."

"Yeah, he gets real crazy and starts yelling and cussing," Chip said.

"He can't stand it if he thinks people are watching him," Lambert said. "He'll be sitting on the front porch and he'll be real quiet and relaxed in the chair and then all of a sudden he'll jump up and start shaking his fists in the air and start cursing over and over again. Then he'll start yelling out, at the top of his lungs, 'G.B.! Why did you do it G.B.?!!!' Then he'll start cussing and cursing G.B., whoever G.B. is."

"Yeah, the guys at the gas station called the cops one night because they thought there was a fight going on and somebody was getting killed," said Chip.

"Sometimes he'll throw the chairs around on the porch—" Jimmy said.

"You guy's are making that up," accused Daniel.

"No they're not," replied Eugene. His refusal to enter in the conversation until now was telling.

"He is pretty spooky, Daniel," Lambert said. "He never says anything to anybody. He just grunts. But ya never know when he's going to get crazy and start screaming and cussing and shaking his fists."

It seemed everyday, rain or shine, hot or cold, midnight or noon, Raymond Wilson was sitting out on the boarding house porch, smoking a cigarette and drinking a cup of coffee. Other than his sudden violent outbursts and uncontrolled shaking and screaming, he appeared to be quite normal.

"Sounds like Dr Jekyll, Mr. Hyde," Daniel said. "Where's he now? I got to see him. Will he chase you if you yell at him-"

"Oh, no you don't," Eugene interrupted. "Don't be making fun of the guy! He's one guy you just don't want to mess with. I'm telling you, man. Believe me. It's not his fault he's nuts. It's that damned war."

Eugene seemed to be warning not only Daniel but all the rest that there were reasons to feel sorry for Raymond. Lambert and Chip's mom told them that some of the neighbors said Eugene's dad had been in Vietnam. Lambert often wondered whether Eugene knew more about his dad than he admitted.

The guys were standing out in the yard when Daniel

motioned with his hand for them to be quiet, "Sssshhhh —
listen!"

"What?" Chip asked.

"Train!" Daniel exclaimed.

"Let's go!" Lambert yelled enthusiastically.

"No, don't! Spike will see us when we cross Hickory Street,"
predicted Jimmy.

"Don't worry about him," Eugene said. "If we go now he
won't see us. He's looking for a burglar."

"Okay," Jimmy explained, "But we'd better watch for my
old man — he was plenty ticked because I slept all day
yesterday."

"What did he say?" Chip asked.

"He said I'd better get some sleep tonight, or he'd come
down here and kick my butt," Jimmy answered. "but he said
'*ass*'.

"Cool, but let's get going. The sun will be up by the time we
get down there!" Eugene reminded them. Equipped with
Daniel's police radio, the five sprinted down the alley and
headed for the train yards. For once Eugene seemed glad that
Daniel was along.

They crossed Powell Street and walked through the alley
behind Goldman's Shoe Store. They hesitated for a moment or
two when they heard a fire truck's siren begin to wail. About
halfway through the alley, Lambert looked up and beheld
Raymond Wilson walking towards them smoking a cigarette.
He was batting at the breezy air with his fist and muttering
something about a "medic" and "Charlies." He shook and yelled
out, "Damned V.C.! Cover him, G.B.!! Ground Cover!! Where
the hell are you G.B.!!" And then he went on a tirade of
expletives.

Even Eugene froze. There was nowhere to go, nowhere to
run, nowhere to hide.

Lambert turned to Daniel and said, "That's him. There's

Raymond."

Daniel ran back through the alley and hid behind the Goldman's building. Jimmy and Chip took off and leapt underneath someone's carport and hid between their car and boat. Lambert guessed he and Eugene thought they were tough or something, but Lambert stood there, motionless behind Eugene. Lambert kept worrying that Eugene would wait too long before doing something.

Raymond was approaching, getting closer and closer, but he abruptly quit shaking his fist and took a long drag off his cigarette as he continued. Lambert could hear his heart pounding in his chest and Eugene breathing next to him. Raymond was mumbling softly to himself, inhaling long drags from his cigarette, and scooting his feet in the gravel as he got nearer and nearer.

Then Lambert heard Daniel's scanner squawk and hiss, a loud voice calling out some license tag, and Jimmy and Chip laughing behind the fishing boat. Eugene turned around and whispered "Shut up guys!"

Raymond began bellowing out an eruption of vulgarities in his deep and raspy voice while feverishly swinging his fists in the air. Eugene grabbed Lambert by the neck and they both began running.

By now Raymond was walking fast, and for once Lambert thought he ran faster than Eugene as they both dove into the Goldman's trash pit which was located underneath the building's fire escape.

Whatever was in those trash bags, it was dead. Lambert even wondered if Scott Lawrence was sleeping in one of them. He and Eugene held their noses and couldn't wait for Raymond to pass so they could breathe again. Yet from this new location they could see Daniel running around in circles in the middle of Powell Street laughing and pointing at Jimmy, Chip, Lambert and Eugene.

Eugene whispered to Lambert, "I'm going to kill him."

Just then Raymond walked by the trash pit smoking his cigarette. He was calm and appeared to be in his right mind as he quietly passed in front of them. As soon as he crossed Powell, Lambert and Eugene bailed out from behind the garbage bags and breathed in fresh air. Chip and Jimmy came straggling down the alley, but before anyone could say anything their attention was drawn back to Raymond who looked like he was having a seizure.

Roaring out a guttural moan like Doctor Frankenstein's creature, Raymond went down on one knee in the middle of Powell Street and shook his fists in the air all the while cussing, cursing, and swearing. Daniel's eyes resembled golf balls as he tripped over himself running away like a scared cat. The others held in their laughs for fear that Raymond would hear them and think they were laughing at him.

Eugene ribbed Lambert and pointed at Daniel who was running down the alley as far away from Raymond as he could get. Raymond then jerkily stood up and lit up another cigarette as he walked in the middle of the street. As he rounded the corner and disappeared behind the corner doughnut shop they laughed when they saw Daniel peeking out from behind a garage.

When everyone regrouped at the camper Daniel yelled at the other four, "Quit making fun of me, guys! You weren't the one face to face with Frankenstein!"

"He was a mile away from you!" Eugene shouted.

"So you, uh, like believe us now, huh?" Jimmy gloated.

"Yeah, but you guys just left me hanging there in the alley! I didn't know where to hide!"

"Ssshhhh! —" Lambert broke in, "There's the train again....it's still coming."

"Let's go to the depot!" shouted Daniel.

"Wait! We'll never catch it at the depot," Lambert declared.

"I got a better idea. Let's go down to the train bridge and watch it cross there!"

"Are you sure?" asked Eugene.

"Okay," Daniel said, "but we ain't crossing the bridge or anything like that."

At that they could all hear the train getting closer as it approached their side of town. They ran along Powell street up to Sixth avenue where they stopped, looked both ways, scanning for cars. Nothing was coming. So they made a break for it.

But just as the five boys bolted across the street, a car engine started and the driver revved the engine. They quickly turned and saw headlights come on and a black and white police cruiser pulled out from a hidden driveway between two houses.

Yelling as they ran wildly across the avenue, the car's engine whined loudly as its tires barked on the concrete. Looking over their shoulders they watched the squad car bounce off the curb, its back end fishtailing in the street as smoke poured forth from its squealing tires.

Jimmy's shoe flew off just as he got to the other curb and it flew back into the middle of the street. He screamed, "My shoe! My shoe, man! We've got to get it."

Lambert felt sorry for Jimmy, but he kept running as hard as he could. Eugene suddenly ran back, grabbed the shoe, threw it to Jimmy, and yelled, "Retard, put your shoe on before the cops catch us."

Running with their feet seemingly ahead of their bodies, except for Jimmy who was hopping with his right shoe in his hand, they rushed over the top of that now familiar hedgerow where they usually sought refuge from passing cop cars. Together they watched in disbelief as the speeding black and white cruiser came around the corner nearly on two wheels. There, just feet away from his face, Lambert beheld two large white numbers painted on the left side of that squad car's jet-black front fender well. They were the numerals seven-seven. Of course, there were no red lights mounted on the top of the car. Yes. It was Spike and his side-kick Goofy. "Son of a —" Lambert said without completing the phrase. He thought to himself how this night could cost him twenty years of his life.

"Tie your shoe while you got the time!" Eugene whispered to Jimmy.

"I can't, man," Jimmy whispered back. "My lace is broken."

"Great," Eugene said as he lowered his face to the ground.

Then the horns of the freight train sounded as it rolled across Sixth Avenue. Eugene whispered from beneath the bushes, "There goes your stupid train. Wish I was on a stupid train. Sure would beat hiding from Spike."

"We're dead—" Jimmy breathed out.

"Speak for yourself," Eugene snapped back, "He ain't caught me yet, and I'll be danged if I let him catch me now and beat me brainless or have Goofy sink his teeth in my hind end. We'll figure a way out."

At that Spike turned his spotlight on and whirled it around shining it up and down the houses and parked cars as he slowly drove down Powell Street. Meanwhile, Lambert hunkered down next to some white petunias and listened and watched as he saw Goofy hanging out the window. Suddenly Goofy began barking loudly and Spike stopped the car, hopped out, and opened the back door to let Goofy out of the cruiser. "Go get 'em, Goof!" said Spike.

Lambert thought they'd all be eaten alive. Eugene was opening his buck-knife in case Goofy attacked him, but a miracle occurred. That jackass of a German shepherd ran over to the other side of the street. Suddenly a cat started screeching and meowing loudly; Goofy growled and barked.

"Goofy — get back in this car!" Spike yelled. "Leave that danged cat alone!" The cat kept meowing as Spike herded Goofy back into the car and slammed the door saying, "We're looking for them juvenile delinquents, Goof! Danged hoodlums!" He got back into his car and drove down to the corner, making a left onto Fifth Avenue.

The boys scrambled to their feet and got their bearings, joyously jumping over the hedges and running wildly down the street so as to avoid encountering Officer Spike again. They began racing each other down Fifth Avenue heading towards the Hickory Street railroad yards. A large Preston Point–Wheatfield Bus crossed Hickory at Bonaventure Boulevard as they sprinted to the tracks.

Lambert yelled, "Go, go!!!"

All of them were laughing and full of glee. They had eluded Spike.

But just as they ran across Hickory into the switchyards, Lambert saw a fast moving black and white police car. Lambert watched as it skidded to a stop, its tires screeching. The squad car made a complete U-turn in the middle of the intersection at Sixth and Hickory and the driver floored the accelerator, squealing the tires, and the red and blue lights came on, flashing brightly. Dust was flying everywhere as the cruiser emerged from a cloud of smoke. The car's engine whined loudly as the patrol car bore down on them.

Eugene was the first to run into the dew-dampened weeds with the others following him. Their feet stumbled across rails and ties, crunching on rock ballast as their bodies swished through the tall weeds of the railroad yard. Lambert froze for a few seconds until Eugene grabbed him by the arm.

"Run!" Eugene yelled. "Head for those freight cars — or else we're busted!" There was nowhere to hide except among the dusty, rusty box cars, gondolas, flats and tankers.

The squad car's headlights and flashing red and blue lights fast approached the boys, flickering and reflecting upon the freight cars, buildings, and upon each of them! Then the cop flipped on his siren for a second or two, perhaps to further intimidate them. Lambert couldn't run fast enough and at that point it became a matter of *every man for himself*. Chip was fifty feet to his right, Jimmy was behind him, Daniel was just to his left, and Eugene — well, Eugene was already hanging on the side of a coal car in the switchyards, climbing it like a grade school kid on the playground monkey bars.

Daniel's scanner squawked, "Car forty-four to headquarters."

"Go ahead car forty-four."

"Yeah, I've got about half a dozen boys running from me on Hickory at the railroad yards! They're probably those hoodlums, or the burglars that seventy-seven is looking for!"

"Car seventy-seven to forty-four," the deep voice of Sergeant Spike boomed in.

"Go ahead."

"Yeah—Goofy and me will be over there in a sec—we'll flush 'em out! I want these guys bad!!"

"Ten-four. Headquarters, send car twenty-two this direction for back-up."

"Headquarters, car twenty-two is clear direct; en route from Saint Clare Avenue!"

"All units, Headquarters clear."

"Oh, Scheis—" Lambert said.

"Son of a pork chop!" Daniel moaned.

"Here he comes, guys – spread out!" Lambert shouted as the scrambled and tripped over themselves in the dark railroad yard at two o'clock in the crazy morning.

"Watch out, here comes another cop!" alerted Daniel as he pointed to the north end of the yards. Sailing down the strip of road was yet another squad car – car twenty-two – doing every bit of eighty miles an hour. The chances of getting out of the mess were nil.

"How the blazes are we going to get out of this one, Lambert?" asked Chip.

"Seriously?" Lambert half-whispered to him as he ran alongside a row of boxcars not knowing what else to say.

"Yeah!" he replied as he darted between two unconnected box cars.

"I'm thinking, man. Don't rush me."

"We'll you better hurry, because this is a real pinch," Chip snapped. "We're cooked man. "Dad will probably ground my butt," Lambert said trying to calm his fears.

"No doubt, camel-breath, but what about my butt?" Chip smarted back, "You and Daniel's great idea to go watch trains! I hope you're getting your fill of them."

At that moment Lambert saw the other speeding police car leave the roadway, jump the curb, and tear into the yards heading straight for them.

"Son of a biscuit! Chip, look!" Lambert exclaimed. "Where's Eugene?"

"Up here, Lammers!" said a voice from above.

Lambert looked up. Eugene was lying on his stomach perched atop a forty foot blue L&N boxcar. "Don't be staring up here guys, or they'll see me. You guys better hide, quick!"

"Where?" Chip nervously asked.

"Who cares where; here he comes!" Lambert eyed a row of blue box cars. "Under a box car!"

Chip crawled under one of the boxcars, out of sight.

Just as the spotlights of the cop car were ready to shine on Lambert, he spotted an open door on one of the boxcars. Lambert made a running jump into the car and struggled to get the lower half of his body up and in. He thought he'd cracked some of his ribs. "Jesus, Mary, and Joseph." He prayed softly to himself as he managed to hide behind the door. Just then the spotlight lit up the inside of the boxcar.

Lambert saw Jimmy and Daniel climbing into an old green Penn Central gondola. Lambert prayed that everybody would escape; not exactly the noblest virtue for which to pray.

Suddenly, as if yet another miracle, Lambert heard what he thought was another train horn. If this were the case, a passing freight train may provide just enough of a distraction for them to run out of the yards and get back home. *Easier said than done.*

Whether it was a southbound or an eastbound, he couldn't be choosy at this point. He'd take what he could get or else he'd be facing off with Goofy and Spike – and a whole lot more.

So here they were. They had three cops closing in upon them coming from three different directions and now there was an approaching train crossing the bridge into town.

That's when Lambert had an idea. It was a chance, a risky gamble, a roll of the dice, but it was all he had between getting busted or getting away home-free. Lambert knew he couldn't keep relying on Eugene to get him out of trouble – (although he had been relying upon him to get him into trouble) – and he wanted to prove that he was just as much a man as Eugene. Yet Lambert had the terrible feeling that one gets when a teacher threatens that all of your failures will go down on your *permanent record*.

Lambert waited for that first long blast of train horns once the engines approached the River Drive crossing. When the train began rumbling over the river, the reverberating sounds of pinging and clanking rails echoed forth as the locomotives clangored across it. Lambert jumped down from the L&N boxcar and climbed up inside the Jimmy and Daniel's gondola half-filled with scrap metal, and called for Chip to get in with them.

"Where's Eugene?" Chip asked as he climbed the hand rails of the Penn Central gondola.

"Eugene's on his own," Lambert answered.

"He's hanging over the top of some tanker car," answered Jimmy.

"Yeah, he's been running along the tops of cars, Lammie." Daniel explained.

Chip was safely in the gondola when a whining car engine that sounded like it was stuck in first gear but going a hundred miles an hour drew their attention.

Peering over the edge of the gondola, they all saw Spike's bald black and white four-door Chrysler – with its five antennas budding from the trunk, two bold white sevens standing out against the jet black fender, and roving spotlight – swiftly snaking its way through the rail yards.

"We got to get out of here!" Jimmy yelled.

"Lambert, let's go!" Chip rejoined.

"Okay guys—here's what we're going to do," Lambert explained, "We'll get out of this gondola and run between the freight cars until we get to the end of the line of boxcars. Then we'll wait for the train. As soon as it gets to the Hickory Street crossing, we'll all run across the tracks—"

"In *front* of the train?" Chip asked incredulously.

"Yeah," Lambert replied. "That's the idea."

"But the cops will see us!" Daniel interrupted.

"Not to mention we could be killed," Chip continued.

"I know, I know, but listen! If we can all get across right before the train crosses the street, then Spike and the other cops will be trapped on the other side of the train giving us just enough time to get back home."

"But what if one of us trips or falls in front of the train?" Jimmy asked.

"You'll probably die," Lambert replied seriously. "That's why no one can afford to trip and fall. Okay? And make sure your shoes are tied. Just pray this is a long train, because if it's just the morning local, we're deader 'n doornails."

"We're going to be dead meat, man. Dead meat." Jimmy said.

"Don't say that!" Lambert said. Suddenly a police car siren began to yelp; it was likely car twenty-two joining in for the kill.

The pitch of the humming train engines decreased as the train began slowing down, beginning its trail through town. The rotating headlights of the oncoming train appeared above the treetops and darkened buildings, the searchlight beams arcing through the muggy air, while crossing signals began to clang and the red warning lamps alternated back and forth. As the air horns began to blast away the boys climbed out of the gondola and jogged between the rows of boxcars and grain cars, hopper cars, and tank cars and alongside the rows of tracks and switches all the while realizing that the cops were closing in on the switchyard.

The refulgent lights of the engine shine on the twin silver ribbons of railheads while the single revolving headlamp washed over them in hooks of light as it painted circles in the sultry sky; the diesel's horns were deafening and constant as the engine crisscrossed multiple grade crossings on its approach to the yards. This light show was enough to rival the Fourth of July fireworks show: the flashing red lights of police cars, crossing signals and crossing gates accompanied by bells, horns, and sirens.

The train was now only seconds away from where Lambert, Chip, Jimmy, and Daniel would have to race across the tracks. Just as they were about to make their dash, there was an incredibly loud bang. Turning to look they saw that the cop who had jumped the curb and had driven through the mud and ruts of the switchyard had tried to run his squad car over two rails that were sticking out from an old spur. His car was stuck; dirt and smoke poured from his spinning back wheels.

Daniel's pocket scanner squawked, "Car forty-four to car seventy-seven!"

"Go ahead, John." Spike angrily answered.

"Spike, get the little bastards! I just tore up car forty-four! Get 'em! They're at Hickory! You got 'em! They're trapped! I think I tore forty-four in half! I can't get it to go in reverse. The transmission's shot or else I broke an axle! Get 'em, and hold 'em for me!!!"

"I'll get 'em for you. They're going to pay for this one!" With that he turned on his siren.

"Aw, man," Chip said, "crossing the train bridge was a cake walk."

With the engineer continuing to blast the engine's horns, the rotating headlight shining on and off the foursome, car seventy-seven quickly approached from behind – Spike and Goofy coming in for the kill. The Chrysler sedan plowed through the weeds; its high beam headlamps, piercing spotlights, wailing siren, and bright red flashing dashboard light adding to the sheer madness.

Less than fifty feet away, the freight train hurtled forward bearing down on the boys, while the engineer relentlessly warned the pedestrians with his horn seeing how the four were way too near the tracks.

"Now!" Lambert yelled, "Run!"

The boys lunged across the tracks to the other side of the roadbed just as the engine was upon them. They turned to look between the passing wheels of the engines and freight cars; Spike drove up to the tracks only to slam on his brakes, raising a storm of dirt and dust as he swerved to miss hitting the train that was now blocking the grade crossing. Spike's siren wailed on.

Then Lambert and the others saw something they'd never forget: Eugene Thomas swinging between two grain cars on the moving train. He climbed around and was dangling on the side of one of the grain cars opposite Spike. But before he was out of sight he had regained his balance and was standing up, swinging freely off the side of that train like a brakeman.

For the moment Eugene had gotten his wish that he was on a train and safely out of Spike's reach. Immediately, though, Lambert regained awareness of his predicament. He and the others ran like they'd never run before. They were laughing and crying at the same time; laughing about Spike being stranded on the other side of the tracks and crying with laughter about the cop who wrecked his car.

Daniel had his scanner up to his ear as he ran along and he said something which brought fear into their hearts. "Spike's calling for the sheriff and the state troopers"

The dreaded state troopers. They made the Preston Point city cops look like wanna-be security guards.

Then horror of horrors – and only halfway home – one by one, Lambert began to hear the bells at the street crossings quit ringing. He turned around and the flashing signals had turned off and the streets were clear! The train was gone! It was only the local freight train, less than thirty cars. As he and the others crossed Fifth Avenue they saw the conductor standing on the end of the blue caboose rolling by with its red lantern blinking.

The Hickory Street crossing was clear! Then Lambert heard what can best be described as the sound like a rocket taking off, but it was only Officer Ron Spike flooring his cruiser's accelerator as he soared over the grade crossing and raced toward them at what looked and sounded like one hundred miles an hour. However his headlights were off, and there was no red light flashing and no siren screaming. He was running blind.

Lambert began to pray again. They ran down the sidewalk and jumped through lawns and gardens. They raced across Sixth Avenue and climbed a couple of fences and hopped over a few hedgerows.

"Oh, great,"Jimmy exclaimed. "I just stepped in dog dung."

"Just keep running," Daniel yelled.

When they got to their neighborhood they ran down the alley, almost home. Yet less than half a block from the camper, where they knew they'd be safe under the blankets, they saw Spike's car speeding down Sixth Avenue going the same direction as they were running. He was going to cut them off at the pass. They heard his tires squealing around the corner. Lambert had come so close only to be nailed in his own backyard.

As they made their way down the alley suddenly a figure appeared from the Weavers' back gate. It was Sonny Sage.

"Oh my Gawd!" Jimmy screamed as he ran past him.

Sonny started panting and screeching like an injured dog and snapped out unintelligible gibberish as the boys ran past him.

Lambert nearly ripped the trailer door off its hinges before diving in; Chip, Daniel, and Jimmy quickly followed in and all of them kicked their shoes off. They made sure the door was shut and locked before getting under the covers. Their faces red and bodies hot from their adventure in hell, or what seemed like hell, they listened in the silence.

"What the hell's that smell?" Jimmy asked.

"It's your shoe, stupid," Chip answered.

"Great, now we have to smell dog dung the rest of the night," Daniel whined.

"Jimmy, hurry up and throw your shoe outside before we all gag and start barfing," Lambert said.

"Good idea." Jimmy opened the trailer door and tossed the shoe outside. As he shut the door, a light came on from behind the trailer.

"Shhh. What's that?!" Jimmy said.

"Our back porch light just came on." Chip said.

"It's three o'clock in the morning! What's your mom or dad want?!" Daniel asked.

"I don't want to know!" Lambert answered. Just then they heard the back door being unlocked from someone inside the house.

"Aw, man. You guys are dead" Jimmy snickered.

Then the door began to creak as they heard the screen door being opened. At that the outside light switch clicked on and the trailer windows facing the house were flooded with light.

"What're the cops saying on the scanner?" Lambert whispered to Daniel.

"I don't know, I haven't heard – Aw, man, it's off!" he whispered loudly as he discovered the problem. "I must've turned it off!!!"

"Why did you do that for?!" Lambert asked, incredulous.

"When I went to turn it down I must've accidentally turned it off."

"Great," Lambert shook his head as he heard the footsteps of an incoming parent. "What're they saying now?"

"Nothing."

"Guys, act like you're asleep." Lambert ordered.

The footsteps stopped and there was a series of soft taps on the door. The silence was shattered with the word, "Boys!" in a loud whisper. It was Mrs. McChesney.

None of them dared say anything. Something had brought her out to the trailer. Lambert could only think of the worst. There was some reason she was outside the trailer door at 3 o'clock in the flipping morning. And Lambert knew it had to be a good reason. And Lambert didn't think it was about Sonny Sage.

"Boys, are you in there?" she asked again as she tapped on the door again, slightly louder this time. So Lambert decided to fake the best waking up voice he could conjure up and top it off with a groggy look, as if they'd been sleeping since midnight. On her third attempt to rouse them, Lambert said, "Huh?…"

"Lambert? Is that you?"

"Wha?…Huh…Ma,…What?"

"Open the door, Lambert."

"Okay," Lambert said as he reached over and opened the door. "What's goin' on Mom?" Lambert said as he squinted in the light as if just rising.

She came in the trailer and shut the door behind her and

began her interrogation, "Are you boys asleep?"

"We were," Lambert said as Daniel, Chip, and Jimmy begin moving under their covers and making customary stretching noises to appear as if they were just waking up as well.

"Have you boys been in the camper all night?" she asked.

Lambert yawned, "Why do you ask?"

"Because I happened to leave my scanner on and around two-thirty the cops started chasing some boys down around the railroad tracks on Hickory street—what's that putrid odor?" Mrs. McChesney paused as she looked at the boys' shoes. "Who's shoes?"

"They're mine, Mrs. M," Jimmy said. "We were out playing some baseball and I must have stepped in dog doo. I'll clean 'em up in the morning."

"You'd better. Your father won't want shoes with dog dung on *his* carpet." Mrs. McChesney paused again and looked around for a second before resuming with her questioning. "Where's that Eugene?"

"Oh, Eugene?" Lambert replied. "Uh, well, uh, he went home around midnight or so."

"Why?" Mother persisted.

"He got mad at Jimmy for stinking up the trailer," Lambert said with a laugh.

"Well, I thought maybe you sneaked out and you boys were the ones being chased by the police. One of the policemen even wrecked his patrol car chasing them."

"No, mom. We were sleeping," Lambert lied as best he could.

"That policeman sure is mad."

Then they all heard the sound of a car coming up the alley. Mrs. McChesney looked out one of the windows. Chip peered out from under the covers and asked, "Who's that?"

She looked at Chip in the darkened trailer and answered, "It's a police car."

Lambert could've died.

She spoke again, "It's one of those unmarked cars."

Now Lambert wanted to die; he knew who that was.

"I wonder what he wants," she said.

*Never mind what, I know **who** he wants,* Lambert thought.

"Is he stopping?" Jimmy nervously asked.

"No, he's just going slow. He doesn't have his headlights on, though. Should I go ask him?"

"No!" came the simultaneous reply from all four boys.

Mrs. McChesney looked at each of the boys but said nothing.

Curiosity got the best of them and all four sat up in bed and peeked out the windows. Sure enough, it was Spike and Goofy, but Spike had his head turned the other direction as they slowly kept going through the alley. As his car cleared the driveway, disappearing behind their garage, and continuing down the block, Lambert had the will to live again. He thanked God, but felt guilty about it.

"Goodnight boys," Mrs. McChesney said. "Now go back to sleep and keep this door locked. You never know, Sonny Sage or those guys the cops are chasing might try to get in the trailer."

"Yeah," Lambert said as he feigned a little laugh as his mother shut the trailer door, turned the outdoor light off and went back in the house.

That was close," Lambert said with a sigh of relief as his mother extinguished the back porch light and darkness once again reigned.

"Where *is* Eugene?!" Chip asked loudly.

"Yeah. How long can a guy hang on to the side of a moving freight train?" Jimmy asked almost as if he didn't want an answer.

"I don't know," Lambert said grimly.

"How fast you think that train can get going?" Chip asked.

"Sixty, seventy — maybe even seventy-five," Daniel

answered.

"Where you think that train is heading?" Chip asked.

"Cincinnati," Lambert answered.

"You think it'll slow down so he can hop off?" Daniel asked.

"Probably," Lambert stammered.

"He may have to hang on for a long time," Daniel whispered loudly.

They all lay in bed recounting the night's adventure, but every little bit Lambert would get sick to his stomach thinking of the many different ways Eugene could die: everything from being scraped off the train going through a bridge or a tunnel, to being caught between two trains on a siding. He worried himself to sleep.

Around nine the next morning, they were awakened by the sunlight and the sound of a westbound freight train.

"Hey, guys, let's go catch that train," Daniel said.

"Yeah, right." Chip said sarcastically as he rolled over in the bed.

"I wonder where Eugene is?" Lambert asked aloud, realizing it was morning.

"Who knows?" Jimmy said, "Knowing him, he's probably hanging on some train bridge somewhere."

"Hey, guys, he did it two nights ago," Chip said, evidently trying to put the others' minds at ease.

"Yeah, but this time he could've bought the big one," Jimmy uttered everyone's fear out loud.

"That's what I'm afraid of," Lambert said under his breath.

In the silence they listened to the birds sing. In the alley they heard Sonny Sage uttering profanities about French fries and Double Cola.

* * * * *

All day long Lambert feared Eugene was dead but Eugene's mother didn't call looking for him. About noon Lambert knocked on her door and she came to the door in her nightgown. He asked if Eugene was back yet and she didn't seem too concerned.

About five o'clock that afternoon the McChesney's doorbell rang. It was Eugene. Eugene told Lambert and Chip how he managed to get away from Spike by running alongside the train before hopping on. He had ridden the train to all the way to Wheatfield before he jumped off. "This morning I hitched a ride on another train going west and I jumped off at the city park!"

Lambert was just glad he was alive.

"'The times are bad! The times are troublesome!'
This is what humans say. But we are our times.
Let us live well and our times will be good.
Such as we are, such are our times. "
- St Augustine

THE END OF AN ERA

Saturday night would be their last night to camp out before school started and though exhausted they were willing to make the sacrifice. Around nine o'clock that night Lambert called Jimmy to find out when he was coming down. Jimmy's dad answered the phone instead.

"Is Jimmy there?" Lambert asked.

"Who is this?" Old Man Wilderman asked.

"Lambert McChesney."

This is one of the McChesney kids," Wilderman asked.

"Yeah, this is Lambert. Chip and I were wondering if Jimmy was going to stay all night with us again tonight?"

"Hell no!" he thundered out, "You been out at all hours of the night, keeping my boy awake, filling his head with Catholic crap, and picking on those roomers next door to you, too, huh? What in the hell did you boys do the past few nights? It sure as hell wasn't sleep, because Jimmy came home every morning and slept all day. He's still asleep!! He didn't even wake up to eat supper! Hell no, he ain't gonna stay up all night again with you and whoever else and that damned Eugene Thomas."

"Oh," Lambert didn't know what else to say.

"Say, we're you the one who woke me up by rattling my damned trash cans? I'll bet that you're one of those hoodlums who caused that cop to wreck his car last night! If you boys are hanging with that group of hoodlums who are out burgling our neighborhood, I'll shoot you! I don't care who you are!" With that he slammed the phone down.

Lambert stood in silence, holding the phone in his hand for a second or two before hanging up. He told Chip about his phone conversation with Old Man Wilderman. Jimmy would definitely not be coming.

Daniel was going to ride his bike over and Eugene said he was coming, but, of course, knowing him, he'd probably show up around midnight.

Chip was tired by the time Daniel arrived. Around twelve-thirty Eugene knocked on the trailer door. Lambert opened the door to see Eugene with a blonde girl in tight jeans and a loose fitting red blouse; the top three buttons of the girl's blouse were opened, revealing her shapely breasts supported by a dainty black bra. She was hanging on his arm and was smoking a cigarette.

"Say, guys," Eugene began, "I can't stay with you tonight. I'll see you round." They walked up the alley. Eugene didn't seem to be himself. The cigarette the girl was smoking looked homemade – and she was sharing it with Eugene.

Chip, Daniel, and Lambert were trying to fight off the drowsiness, but they couldn't keep their eyes open. They collapsed on the beds in the trailer and fell asleep, still wearing their shoes.

In the middle of the night Lambert woke up and slowly removed Chip's glasses from his face, took his shoes off, covered him with a blanket, and kissed him on the cheek. Here they were together, just the three them. The day's heat gave way to a cool night breeze and it felt good. Lambert smiled, rolled over, said a prayer and fell asleep.

The next morning Lambert and Chip's mom woke them up early so they could come in, shower, and get ready for church.

Summer vacation was over and before they knew it they were back in school.

* * * * *

That fall Lambert got a job at *The Pancake Palace* and spent more and more of his time working. Eugene soon drifted out of their lives and out of the neighborhood. Lambert would see Eugene here and there as one does in a small town, but it was never the same as the summer of 1981.

In many ways it was a turning point in Lambert's life, indeed for all of their lives, a matter of growing up and experiencing death – the death of relationships and inevitable change.

When Lambert was a kid he had all the time in the world. As he grew older it was as if time went faster and faster. He wondered if the closer one got to death, the closer one got to eternity—the ever-present moment when chronological, sequential time exists no more. And, if so, then is eternity where we will all finally find the time to do all those things that we never had the time to do?

Thinking back, Lambert really wondered what the cops would have done to them had they caught them. The boys may have actually served a good purpose—keeping the cops on their toes.

Lambert also had some time to think about that "permanent record" of which teachers always remind their students. Has anybody ever seen one? How many people's bosses have fired them because they chewed gum in class, threw spit wads, or pounded the erasers on the side of the school building?

Not that anyone would encourage that kind of behavior, of course, but do permanent records really exist? And if they do, who sees them and where are they kept, in some huge federal building? Or in the case of Catholic schools, are they kept in some convent basement or monastery library? That would have been a great question for the guys to have talked about and philosophized over during one of those famous all-nighters in the trailer through the wee hours of some summer morning hours near the corner of Bonaventure and Powell.

Ah, to be young again and stay out all night with the guys. Those were the days.

*"The confession of evil
is the beginning of good works."*
– Saint Augustine

Epilogue

In Lambert's senior year of high school, Lambert, Chip, and Jimmy went over to *The Pancake Palace* one winter evening. They sat in a booth, drank hot chocolate, and shared stories of those summer nights in the trailer and the train yards and other follies; they laughed till they cried.

Jimmy explained that Eugene had gotten mixed up in alcohol and drugs in the past year or so. Not only that but he dropped out of school after Wendy Smith got pregnant even though rumor had it that he wasn't for sure that it was his child.

It's funny how life and time does seem to move more and more quickly the older you get There's no one left in the neighborhood, the rail yards are empty, the rails rusty and abandoned, the ties warped and dry, the depot torn down, the *Pancake Palace* boarded up, and the cops are either retired or dead.

On a recent trip to his hometown of Preston Point, Lambert drove through town and saw a political sign in someone's yard: Ron Spike for Mayor. Lambert smiled and laughed. And it was then that he knew that in Preston Point some things never change.

Lambert drove around his old block and went down the alley. There was no Chip, no Eugene, no Jimmy, no Daniel, and no ball game on the sandlot. Old Man Wilderman, Merle and Mabel Weaver, and Sonny Sage had long since died. One of the homes had burned down and the rest of the houses looked as if they should be torn down. Lambert rounded the block and saw the empty lot where *The Burger Place* used to stand and passed the old doughnut shop which is now closed. As he turned the corner, he beheld a familiar slumped figure of a man ambling the street. It was Scott Lawrence. His beard was salt and pepper, his eyes tired, and his clothes still mismatched and fashionably frumpy.

Lambert drove to the river and parked near the railroad bridge and sat for a while. To his surprise a passing freight train crossed the bridge. In his mind's eye he saw Eugene climbing the bridge and Jimmy weeping over an old athletic shoe.

Sunset

The stoplights flash silently,
alternating yellow and red
steadily, constantly,
ever constantly changing.
A tavern's neon sign flickers away
light from the streetlamps
filters through the leaves
casting shadows
upon a silent empty street.

Nighthawks dart and dive
the Vesper Sparrows
and the robins
all voice their delight
in evening twilight
till there's no more light.
The sounds of crickets and locusts fill the night
countless stars reveal themselves
in a blue-black heaven

A melancholy blue moan of a train
a lonely freight voices its advent
announcing its arrival in town
its accompanying clamor and cacophony
dispels the hush of night and the citizen's slumber

That late August sound of cicadae whining into the night,
the sun going down earlier and earlier every evening
ever reminded us that summer was at its end
and school would be
starting once again.

Afterword

Perhaps growing up in the Midwest afforded me the luxury of taking life at a more leisurely pace, and in the process I had the chance to study life around me perhaps a bit closer than others. Of course, no writer writes in a vacuum, so many of the stories in this novel are formed out of the primordial clay of my memory and my own life. The characters and situations have been fashioned to tell a story; names have been changed to protect the guilty. Of course, the names, characters and incidents depicted in this book are products of my imagination and any resemblance to actual events or persons, living or dead, is entirely coincidental.

In no way, shape, or form am I encouraging my young readers to go out and try any of these antics or shenanigans in their own town or city, but adolescent boys are always going to stretch the boundaries in an attempt to carve out their own identities.

The story entitled *The Sinister Plot* is loosely based on a real event, but it would be several years later when I would read Saint Augustine's *Confessions* and discover that he and his companions had stolen a neighbor's pears only to throw them at pigs. Augustine relates that all it took was for one of their number to say, "Come on; let's do it," and the deed began. He maintains that he and his companions stole the pears not because they were hungry or because the pears were particularly succulent; they didn't even steal them to give to the poor. They stole them because it was forbidden to do so.

So it was with Lambert. He stole the tomatoes for the thrill of throwing them at cars. And in the colloquial terms in use during the 1980s – he, like Augustine of old, threw the fruit at a pig.

Eugene and the Haunted Train Bridge and the subsequent Close Encounters in the Rail Yard are a hodge-podge of near occasions of sin. The metaphysical dialogue between the characters, the mixture of sin and grace, and the habitual running to and fro are indicative of human nature.

In the words of the humorist James Thurber, "Before they die, all human beings should try to learn what they are running from, and to, and why."

John William McMullen
6 January 2010
The Feast of the Epiphany

About the Author

John William McMullen, a student of philosophy, theology, and history, holds a Master's Degree in Theological Studies, is a Theology Instructor, College Philosophy Professor, Third Order Benedictine Oblate affiliated with Saint Meinrad Archabbey in Indiana, and a Permanent Deacon for the Catholic Diocese of Evansville. His publishing credits include historical works, novels, novellas, short stories, and political and religious articles. He is currently working on another novel.

He may be contacted at: johnmcmullen@insightbbb.com

Other Works by John William McMullen

The Last Blackrobe of Indiana and the Potawatomi Trail of Death
(The story of Rev. Benjamin Petit and the Indiana Indian Removal of 1839)

ROMAN
(The trial of the Rev. Roman Weinzaepfel in 1840s Indiana)

Utopia Revisited:
A 21st Century Account of a Diplomatic Visit to the Island Nation of Utopia

POOR SOULS
A Year in the Life of an American Catholic Seminarian
Set in the late 1990s

The Miracle of Stalag 8A:
A Beauty Beyond the Horror
Olivier Messiaen and the "Quartet for the End of Time"

**For other books published by
Bird Brain Productions,
Check our website at:
www.birdbrainproductions.com**

Recently released:

Odd Numbers
by
M. Grace Bernardin

"Touching, clever, and at times delightfully off the wall, Odd Numbers is a gulp of fresh air. Bernardin's characters are like us - flawed but hopeful." - **Mike Whicker, author of** *Invitation to Valhalla* **and** *The Blood of the Reich.*

Is it possible to find love in the heart of the Midwest between a strip mall and a cornfield? This is the quest of three friends who meet in the 1980s at the Camelot Apartments located amidst the suburban sprawl of the southern Indiana town of Lamasco. Odd Numbers spans twenty years and ultimately culminates with the startling collision that reconnects the three friends.